Fate in the Sunrise

A SHIFTER ROMANTIC SUSPENSE

CHARLENE PERRY

CHARLENE PERRY

CHAPTER 1

Property

Some days, I love my job.

Today is not one of those days. I push the latch on the centrifuge for the fifth time, finally hearing a click. It's perfectly safe once the locks are engaged, but the ancient machine has to put up a fight every damn time.

When I accepted the offer to work as a lab tech at BioSol, it wasn't exactly the career path I'd dreamt of. But cutting-edge, off-world tech and life on the cusp of innovation would make up for the compromise, right?

Cusp of innovation. Sure. On the other side of the compound, maybe. Here in my little wing, it might as well be a country clinic. Which would suit me just fine if it included promiscuous house cats, doe-eyed children with new puppies, and orphaned farm animals. A country clinic would be a dream. It *was* my dream.

I shake my head and down the last of my cold coffee.

R&D at BioSol was my father's legacy, lost to the illness that stole his memories. But even with his fractured mind, the moment I mentioned the offer for a lab tech position, his eyes lit up. He started telling stories he hadn't recalled in years. No amount of aging equipment or childhood dreams will keep me from fulfilling the promise I made to him that day; I will earn my way to take his place as head of the Shifter program.

While today might feel like a step in the wrong direction, the fact is that I've worked my ass off and everything is going exactly to plan. Straight out of high school, I completed three years of pre-vet in almost half the time. Then, four years to earn my DVM. From there, I went straight to work here at BioSol as a lab tech. Four years later, I'm head of my department. At twenty-eight years old, I'm on track to be the youngest addition to the Shifter R&D program.

And yet, when one of my techs calls in sick at the last possible minute, I'm still the one taking temperatures and fighting with the ancient equipment. I would never complain out loud, though. While BioSol might be stingy with granting my equipment requests, they are certainly not stingy with my salary.

A warbled chime announces my last appointment of the day. When everything else fails, at least time keeps moving. Focusing on that thought gives me the inspiration I need to paste a smile on my face and greet my four o'clock.

"Hello, Agent..." Shit. I grab my tablet and swipe the screensaver. "Agent Bates. What can I do for you today?"

I look up from the screen, and Agent Jon Bates is smiling from the doorway. It's the kind of smile only an Agent can pull off. That cocky, you-know-you-want-me smirk.

As impressive as he is with his implant tattoos, badass tactical gear, and the sleek cheetah Shifter at his side, he's so not my type.

"My cat needs a tune up." He crosses his arms, and even though I'm not into him in a general sense, I'm definitely checking out the impressive display his biceps are putting on.

"What's your concern?" I turn my attention to the cheetah, who's looking around the room. He's relaxed, no obvious signs of agitation or illness.

"He's acting weird. I want a full diagnostic, or whatever you do. If he's losing his edge, I need to know. I can't afford to be on a mission and have him less than one hundred percent."

I nod like any of that is at all helpful. "We can run some bloodwork and order an MRI. See if there's anything amiss. How does that sound?"

"It's a start. When do I pick him up?"

"Oh no, you can stay. Shifters tend to get a bit nervous here. He'll want you close."

He laughs, a condescending tone that makes me inwardly cringe. As if my suggestion that his Shifter might have an opinion on the matter is somehow beneath him.

"If he needs a mother, that's not what I signed up for. I think he can handle himself."

I flinch as he swats the side of the cheetah's head, drawing the Shifter's attention. "Do as you're told, cat. I hear you disobeyed this lovely woman, and I'll make sure you regret it."

"He'll be fine," I assure him, not that I have any clue. I've never had an Agent leave their Shifter with me. "We'll be finished in under thirty minutes."

"Sounds good."

"What's his name?"

He smirks. "Just call him Cat."

Agent Bates leaves without a backward glance, and I'm left with a full-grown cheetah Shifter that looks equally unaffected by their separation.

The poor creature.

Shifters live for the bond they share with their Agents. This cheetah would have been just a kitten when he was matched with Agent Bates.

I crouch down in front of him, my heart skittering just a little. He might look passive now, but this is no ordinary animal. Shifters are intelligent, able to think and reason and even speak through the Link implant they share with their Agents. They can shift into the forms of other animals, reason through complex situations, and are deadly weapons when the situation calls for it.

"Hey, hon." He doesn't respond or even look at me. "Cat?"

No response.

"I'm going to put my hand on the back of your neck to feel for any swelling around your implants, okay?"

Still nothing. I reach toward him, and while I'm rarely hesitant around Shifters when their Agents are standing close by, my hand trembles just a bit as I thread my fingers through his lush fur. I dig down to the skin, feeling the lean, bunched muscle of his neck. As I press over the spine where his implants would be, his eyes drift closed.

"Everything seems fine. I'd like to check your eyes now. Can you look at me?"

He ignores my question for a moment, then glances at me briefly before looking back at the wall.

"I know eye contact is uncomfortable, but can you please look at me?"

His big, round, soulful eyes finally lock on mine. They're a deep golden and filled with so much intelligence I find it hard to believe I'm looking at an animal.

"Hey there. You're safe with me, okay?"

He slow blinks, and I get the feeling he's trying to act like he doesn't understand me. His eyes drift away, but I do something I know I shouldn't do; I put my hand on the side of his face.

He flinches, but holds my stare as I stroke his soft cheek with my thumb.

This is already crossing a professional line, but I don't care. I'm going to speak my mind. This poor creature deserves a little self-esteem boost.

"The way he treats you isn't right. I hope you know that. You're so much more than just a tool to be used. You deserve better."

Shifters don't like to be touched by anyone other than their bondmates. They don't respond to being spoken to by anyone else, either. But I'm guessing this boy doesn't get a lot of physical affection or casual communication from his Agent. He doesn't seem to mind my touch and my affirmation has him leaning into my hand ever so slightly.

I feel a brief twinge of something in my chest at the small connection I've made with this incredible creature, and I keep my hand on him as I take his vitals, hoping it offers some comfort.

He doesn't take his eyes off me as I finish the last of my assessment and return to my desk to label the vials he let me draw from his forearm.

Shifters terrify me, despite my chosen career. They're enigmas. Alien embryos shipped in from off-world to be implanted in wolves, bears, or big cats. Bonded with Agents within a few weeks of birth, they grow at an accelerated rate, forming their personality and morals from their human counterpart's own experiences and beliefs. They're the perfect partner; the perfect weapon.

But Cat doesn't feel like an alien. If anything, he feels human.

That's a dangerous thought. I've seen what happens when a Shifter starts to feel a little too human. A lab tech was in the ICU for weeks after he was attacked by a Shifter in human form. They can't handle a human mind or human emotions. It makes them violent. Insane. Which is why it's illegal, and any Shifter caught attempting it is put down immediately.

The door creaks open and Cat looks away. I hadn't even realized I was holding his gaze while my mind was wandering.

"Hey, Fate." Matthew pokes his head in, doing a quick scan to make sure we're alone in the cluttered little exam room. "Agent Asshole is in the waiting room."

I just shake my head, trying not to laugh at the client's expense.

"You met Agent Bates?"

He snorts. "Yeah, and it seems like you made quite an impression on him. At least, your ass made quite an impression on him."

I roll my eyes. "Well, you know how my dating life's been lately..."

He points a finger at me, his eyes as stern as a big brother's. "You'd be better off dating his Shifter. That man's lower than an animal."

I laugh at his unnecessary warning, but at the same time, I meet Cat's unrelenting stare. I wonder what he'd look like in human form? What would he say about his life or his future? Would he be cocky like Bates once he had a voice and a man's body, or would he be as gentle and thoughtful as he seems in this form?

Good lord. Maybe it has been too long since I went on a date.

Matthew pushes the door open wider, his six-foot-seven frame blocking the gap. He's a Protector, like Agent Bates, but a lower rank. Enforcers don't get matched with Shifters, but in exchange they seem to retain a personality. Maybe that's just Matthew. He's got personality to spare.

"Want me to walk him out?" He gestures at Cat, and my heart sinks at the idea of sending him back to that man.

"No, just send him in."

"If you insist." He pauses mid turn, slapping his hand on the door frame for emphases. "I won't be far if you need backup."

I wave off his concerns, though I'm always grateful to have Matthew on duty nearby.

A few minutes later, Agent Bates strolls in like he's here to pick up his dry cleaning. I suspect he'd have more respect for the clothing.

"You done, sweetheart?"

Gross. I don't react to the nauseating endearment.

"I am. We should have the results within a week, but I'm sure everything is fine. He seems quite healthy."

"Healthy." He scoffs. "It's not his physical I'm concerned about, but you know the drill. Gotta pass this test first."

He pats his leg, actually pats his leg like he's calling a dog.

Thankfully, he turns away so he doesn't see me fuming when Cat obediently heeds the call.

It's silly to feel this way. Regardless of the intelligence brimming in the depths of those wide eyes, he's far from human. He's Agent Bates' property, and their relationship is none of my business.

CHAPTER 2

Consequences

I jump at the shrill sound of a car's horn in the distance, and I can't help but laugh at myself. Standing on my front step in the dark, I've been lost in thought as the chill and drizzle soak into my clothes and turn my hair into a frizzy disaster.

I just can't get my mind off that cheetah. The poor soul doesn't even have a name. They're bondmates, for heaven's sake. How does that not mean something?

I've seen many variations of the bond. Most Agents genuinely care about the comfort and well-being of their Shifters. Some take it a step further, and they're more like family. You'd never guess they're talking about an animal when they speak about their loyal sidekick. Others are less personally attached, more like the typical working animal and owner relationship. A few are like Agent Jon Bates, detached and uncaring. Agent Bates takes the prize for most awful, though.

He doesn't even have a name.

I shake my head and turn the key. I don't bring work home. It's a self-care rule I won't break. I can work an 18-hour day if needed, but once I step into my home, I won't spare another thought for that cat.

A rustle of branches draws my attention to the neatly trimmed rose bushes sheltering my door, and then I'm frozen in place with my hand on the unopened latch.

It's him. The cheetah. My heart's beating out of my chest as I'm caught in his golden stare. Why would he...

I snap my head around, looking for inky tactical gear and a cocky smirk. It's beyond inappropriate that Agent Bates would think he could follow me here.

Cat steps toward me, further into the halo of light from my porch. There's something different in the way he's looking at me, a confidence that wasn't there before. I take a deep breath. There's no reason to be afraid. I'm sure there's a perfectly good explanation for this.

"What are you doing here?"

His lean body bends, reshaping, and in one fluid movement the cheetah's gone and a man stands in his place.

I can't move. I can't speak.

He takes a step toward me, and even though there's a rational voice inside my head telling me to run, to scream, to hit him with a dose of pepper spray...

His eyes pin me like a stunned rabbit. I'm helpless under the intensity of his stare. His cheetah's eyes were golden, but as a man they're a shade of brown, flecked with that same gold tone. That same searching intelligence.

"How are you... what are you..."

His eyes drop to my mouth as his tongue darts out to moisten full lips. He's attractive. Objectively. His face is angular but not severe, his eyes soft and his dark hair tousled in that messy yet somehow stylish way some men can pull off. He's tall and broad and he's wearing a simple shirt that hugs impressive biceps and clings to his obviously defined chest.

I force my eyes back up to his.

"What am I?"

His question comes out on a breath, but I nearly jump out of my skin. This is wrong. He's a Shifter. They can't do this. His mind can't handle the vastness of a human brain, human emotions... he's going to snap and murder me while I'm checking him out. Maybe I'm the one who's losing my mind.

"You can't do this. It's not... you're not..."

Dammit. Why can't I form sentences? Maybe I'm in shock.

"I needed to see you." He inches closer, cautiously, like he's as wary of me as I am of him. "I've never thought about... more. But your voice, your touch."

Images of those Shifters from the lab flash in my mind, their eyes wild and unfocused as they lashed out against a world they couldn't comprehend. Cat's eyes look nothing like theirs, as his searching gaze holds me captive, pleading for answers I simply can't give.

How is this possible?

He reaches out, and I hold my breath as he touches my hand, sending shock waves across my skin. I swallow the urge to question how this happened, why he attempted such a thing, what's going through his mind right now... I want to know everything about him, but I'm not at the lab and nothing about this is safe for him or me.

A car downshifts as it passes and I pull away, refusing to feel bad at the rejection I see so clearly in his eyes. But the light traffic is moving along like usual, no one caring about the seemingly ordinary scene playing out on my front porch.

What have I done?

I took pity on him when it was none of my business, and I crossed a line. I engaged, communicated, connected with him. And now he's spiralling into an existential crisis that's going to get him killed and me fired.

"You have to go back to your Agent. This is... inappropriate." I take a deep breath and summon more confidence into my tone. "I'll contact him, if that helps."

His eyes close, and he moves his head from side to side. "I

can't."

My heart aches for him. For the way his Agent treats him, and for the way he's looking at me now, like I hold the answers.

The neighbor's houses have lights on inside, but we're mostly sheltered from view. It's unlikely anyone would have seen him shift. But I saw him. I have to report this, don't I? It's too risky to keep what I've seen to myself.

"Please. You have to leave. I won't tell anyone if you go now."

I'm not certain I can keep that promise, but if it helps convince him to walk away...

He steps closer. Oh lord. I need to end this interaction, but I can't risk him following me inside. It's far safer out here than in the privacy of my home.

I could bolt for my car. Maybe the sudden action would catch him off guard and he wouldn't react in time to catch me. But the truth is, while everything about this situation is terrifying, I'm not actually afraid of *him*. Maybe the way he looks is short circuiting my survival instincts, but I don't honestly think he'd hurt me.

Holding my breath, I turn the handle and push inside, knowing full well he can muscle his way through if he chooses.

"I can't go back."

Just lock the door. Call his Agent, the Protectors, my boss, anyone. I made a mistake, but I can fix it.

I can hear him breathing. In my mind, I see the rise and fall of his chest, his breaths coming faster as he looks over his shoulder. He's afraid.

Fuck.

What am I doing? I don't need to understand this, and I certainly shouldn't be feeling compelled to help him. Letting him in my house would be reckless and stupid and...

I slowly open the door, and one glance at the look on his face has me swinging it wider.

He doesn't move, and I can't form words. I lower my eyes from his and move aside.

CHAPTER 3

Dangerous

I finally work up the courage to move closer, smoothing my damp hair as I venture with measured steps toward the centre of my living room.

Two plush chairs and a curved, white sofa surround a low, round table. During the day, the floor-to-ceiling windows bathe the space in natural light, my favorite feature when I happily paid twenty percent above market value for this cozy, modern little house in a quiet neighbourhood.

At this moment, I'm particularly grateful for the light-sensing curtains that close as the sun sets. I've never liked coming home to the feeling that someone might be watching me through the glass, and I'm certainly glad for the privacy now.

Unless the Shifter in the body of a man snaps and murders me.

After I exercised my epically poor judgement and let him inside, he walked calmly around the open concept kitchen and living room. He touched the grocery list hanging on the fridge, and the coffee mug drying beside the sink. He ran his fingertips along the spines of the books on my shelf.

Once he'd made a full loop around, looking at everything and touching anything that seemed to catch his eye, he settled onto the white sofa with his arms resting on his knees and his eyes fixed on the floor between his feet.

I venture to sit on the edge of the chair opposite him, and he lifts his head just enough to look up at me. Damn if my heart doesn't flutter when his eyes meet mine.

My survival instincts are clearly misfiring. I've willingly let a predator into my house. He could shift into any number of deadly creatures. A dragon even, if he's learned that form. Though to be fair, most Shifters never learn purely mythical creatures. I can't say a grizzly would be any less destructive.

"You can't stay here. You can't stay... like this."

"I know."

Something about the look in his eyes as he says those words makes my racing heart drop to my stomach and settle like a brick.

"Did you know?" His words are edged with gravel, his voice heavy with the emotion I can read as clear as day in his searching eyes.

I shake my head, but I'm not even sure what I'm denying. "You can't take human form. It's physically possible, yes, but your mind won't survive it. I've seen the aftermath. I've seen Shifters in human bodies and they're... they can't handle it."

"Then why do I feel like I can think clearly for the first time?" He reaches his hand out, running his fingertips along the edge of the low coffee table like the smooth pine finish fascinates him. "Jon does his job, he lives his life, and I'm... just there. But everything around me has a purpose now. It has meaning."

I swallow the lump in my throat. He's speaking in complete sentences, expressing his thoughts and desires as articulately as any human would. I don't understand why, but he's different somehow.

The others I've seen at BioSol, though there were only two that I witnessed personally, they tore at their hair and writhed like they were in pain. Cat doesn't look at all uncomfortable in his human form. Just defeated and confused about his place in the world.

"What's your name?"

His eyes snap to mine at the simple question, and a smile plays at the corner of his mouth. I refuse to let my traitorous eyes follow the slight movement. It's perfectly normal for me to find him attractive, that's just biology. It doesn't mean I need to act on it or even think about it.

"My name is Chase."

"Agent Bates said-"

"Jon doesn't use that name."

He leans back on the sofa, and I focus on my hands in my lap rather than the way his jeans hug his thighs as his shirt lifts to show the smallest sliver of skin at his trim waist.

"Two years back, we were on basic patrol at a festival."

I peek over at him, but his eyes are distant as he recalls the memory.

"I found a girl, a tiny little thing, lost and cowering in a corner. Jon kept moving, said it wasn't our concern. But she wasn't scared of me. She looked me right in the eyes and talked to me like... like a person. She told me her entire life story, which wasn't very long. Put her little arms around me, and I stayed with her until she was found. She named me Chase because cheetahs are fast. She said if she could run as fast as me, she'd never stop. Maybe she was on to something. Maybe that's what I should be doing."

I take a deep breath, keeping my focus on the logical outcome of this situation and not allowing my tugging heartstrings to dictate my response. "Running's not the answer. You don't know how much longer you can sustain this without consequences. If you turn yourself in to BioSol..."

"I've called myself Chase in my head ever since. Jon thought it was ridiculous. I slept on the garage floor for weeks after suggesting he use it."

I shiver at the thought. Animal, Shifter, person, whatever. There's no excuse for being cruel to another living thing.

There was no denying cat's... Chase's... intelligence even before he looked like this. Bates had the ability to listen and talk through their Link implant all along, so he had to have known his Shifter was more than just a simple animal.

"Does he ever..." I choose my words carefully. The last thing I want to do is touch on something that will make him angry. "Does he ever punish you physically when you upset him?"

I saw how casually he struck the side of Chase's head at the lab. It was hard to witness, but neither one of them reacted like it was out of the ordinary.

"Jon doesn't want me talking or acting like I'm more than I am. He puts me in my place when I overstep."

Tears sting at the back of my eyes as I picture that beautiful creature being abused. I stand up from the chair, going to the kitchen for a glass of water so he can't see how affected I am by the thought of him living that life.

"I have a Medic implant, so I heal fast. It's never been a problem."

But it is a problem. I can't walk away and pretend this never happened. If I turn him in to BioSol, will they see how natural this form is for him or will they follow the law and euthanize him without ever giving him the chance to speak for himself? His short life has been a tragedy. I can't bear the thought of this being how it ends.

I can't get involved any more than I already am, but maybe there is one thing I can do to give him a fighting chance.

"You can't stay here, but there's someone I want you to meet. Someone who might have answers. Would you be up for that?"

"Fuck, yes."

I nearly laugh at his enthusiastic answer, but it quickly dies in my throat when I turn to find him standing inches from me.

I set my glass down, bracing myself on the edge of the island. I should back away to a safer distance, but I can't resist taking in his features close-up in the crisp interior light. Did he choose these details when he took this form? How much was instinctual and how much was preference?

I see a faint resemblance to Agent Bates, but his eyes are entirely his own. His hair is nothing like Bates' short cut. His body is clearly defined under jeans and a shirt that he would have conjured along with all the rest.

I jolt when his fingers touch my face, then trail along my cheek. His eyes track the movement as he seems mesmerized by tracing the curve of my jaw, the edge of my bottom lip.

I step back, because while his touch seems purely inquisitive, it's doing crazy things to my body. I should not be turned on by him. This is a purely scientific opportunity. The chance to learn something about another species that might not have been known before now.

And maybe help Chase find a better future.

I clear my throat. Pushing away any thought that isn't expressly professional.

"Come back on Saturday. I want to take you to see my father."

Chase's eyes light up, that almost-smile returning to play at the corners of his mouth.

"He's retired and his memories are... intermittent, but he was head of the Shifter R&D program at BioSol for years. He might have some insight on what's happening to you." And some guidance for me, as I'm sure he'll understand the precarious position I'm in.

Chase's smile is everything as he nods his agreement, and heaven help me if my heart doesn't burst wide open.

Growing up, I took in any injured or stray animal that crossed my path. I couldn't resist, no matter how dire their chances of survival, they were all my babies. That old feeling's back full force when I look at Chase and he looks at me, although it's anything but maternal.

I wish it were that platonic. But just as strong as my sudden need to help him is the urge to get closer, to feel that spark that lit my skin when he touched me on the porch and again moments ago.

It's that feeling that makes this far more dangerous than nursing any wild animal back to health.

CHAPTER 4

Clever Dog

"She's going to be running that place soon, you'll see." Dad's eyes glimmer with pride as he finishes his slightly exaggerated description of my current and future role at BioSol. "With my last name, she's got it made."

Dad took great pride in his work at BioSol, and I know he had a hand in their decision to approach me. Even though I'd always rebelled against his hopes for my future, watching him lose his career to this illness put a lot of things into perspective.

I might be nowhere near running the show yet, but he's right. I'll get there. The Carter name is well-respected at BioSol because of his work. Carrying on that legacy is the least I can do for the man that raised me.

I glance up at Chase, and he raises an eyebrow.

I roll my eyes at Dad's praise, which earns a smirk that's a little too sexy on a man who walks on four legs most of the time. Whatever's happening is unnatural and dangerous, but I'm not blind. I can appreciate that he looks like he belongs on the cover of a romance novel, but that doesn't change what he is.

He's a Shifter. Enough said. I caught myself zoning out in a daydream featuring him too many times in the three days since he was first in my house, and that just makes this situation all the more dangerous. I need to figure out what to do. An option that doesn't involve sneaking around with a ticking time bomb of insanity.

Because Chase is under my skin, that I can't deny. He's consuming my thoughts when I should be focused on work, and he's tugging at my heart in a way that assures me there's no turning back now. I need to help him. I want to help him.

"Dad, can I ask you a question about Shifters?"

He tips his chin up, his cloudy eyes darting between Chase and me.

"Have you ever known one to take human form and adapt?"

He snorts, his gaze drifting off to the side and taking on that distant look he gets when his thoughts have wandered away from the present.

I reach over, placing my hand on his knee where he sits in the faded armchair he's had since before I was born. He refused to move into the long-term care facility without it, and the nurses tell me he gets them to move it out to the common area when he wants to socialize.

"Dad, please. I know you can't talk about most of the work you did there. But you were head of the Shifter program. Can some of them adapt to human forms?"

I watch his face for any acknowledgement that he understands what I'm asking him, but there's nothing. He's drifted off to some place far from here.

Chase moves closer, and I hear him crouch down next to my chair.

"What can I do?"

The concern in his voice makes my eyes sting. I pinch the bridge of my nose, refusing to give in to the emotions threatening to make this a pity party.

It's hard to see my father like this. He used to be so alive, so passionate about his work. Even the parts he couldn't talk about, he would still find ways to weave stories about his day that amazed me. I still see glimpses of that man now and then, but they never last for long.

"He's the only person I can trust with this. He has to know something."

Heat sears my thigh through my jeans as Chase's hand settles firmly on my leg. Every coherent thought and emotion is wiped away as my reality reduces to that single point of contact.

He's a Shifter. He's an animal, not a human. Just because the form he's wearing now is visually appealing doesn't mean I should be reduced to a melting puddle of hormones from just one touch.

"I could show him?"

His words jolt me out of my haze. I move my leg to get some distance, and he seems to take the hint as he drops his hand.

I clear my throat, hoping Chase can't sense the way my body reacts to him. "I don't want to scare him, but maybe?"

"No surveillance here?" He looks around, checking the corners of the room.

"No. It's private."

He stands, and I reach to take my father's hand.

"Dad, Chase has something to show you."

He moves to within my father's view, and I gently squeeze the frail hand, hoping he's not totally lost to reality.

Chase shifts, the transition nearly instantaneous as he seems to melt from human into feline. When his yellow cat-eyes meet mine, the same heat flares as when he touched me. I look away, focusing on Dad. I'll dissect my entirely inappropriate reaction to *a cat* later.

Dad's focused on Chase. At first, he doesn't appear to react, but his eyes slowly widen. The hand I'm holding grips mine with surprising strength as his mouth opens and closes with silent words.

"Dad?"

He shakes his head, his eyes never leaving Chase. He's not breathing. Oh, shit! "You need to go."

What the hell did I do?

I take his face in my hands, telling him everything's okay as the door closes behind Chase, leaving us alone.

"Dad, you're okay. You're good."

"It didn't work." His words are barely audible, but he shakes his head and pushes my hands away. "It didn't work."

"Dad, please, what didn't work?"

"The incompetent fools!"

The force of his statement is startling, but I breathe a sigh of relief at the clarity in his gaze and his steady breaths. I should have anticipated that could be too much for him to handle.

I move back to my seat beside him, and he turns his head to hold my stare. There's nothing distant in his eyes now. He's here and he's pissed off, but I can't help but feel grateful for the glimpse of the man he used to be.

"What are you saying, Dad? Tell me. I need to understand why Chase can do what he's doing."

"It's not natural. We tried to cut it out of them. I almost had it, but the fools couldn't do it without me."

"I don't understand..."

"Inhibitors, gene therapy, transplants, lobotomy." He presses his fingers to his temples, shaking his head in frustration. "Nothing works. The shifting always came back. We don't need them to *think*, we need them to *obey*. I was almost there. A stronger subject, one who could survive the procedure, that's all I needed."

His words hit me like a gut punch. I can't believe what I'm hearing. But as disjointed as his statements are, his eyes meet mine with steady determination.

"They're animals. They shouldn't be allowed to take our form and live beside us."

I swallow past the lump in my throat. "But you're saying they can. They always could. We just don't want them to." I think I might be sick.

Shifters can do what Chase is doing naturally. It's humans who've turned them into... into property. This is what my father did. This is what BioSol does.

"Dad, no. This can't be true."

He grips my arm and I gasp at the strength of it.

"They can't be allowed to take human form. He needs to be put down before others see."

I shake my head. Something doesn't add up... I saw it with my own eyes; Shifters driven mad with the effort of sustaining a human mind. Or maybe it does add up, only the alternative is simply too disgusting to imagine.

I pull out of his grip, nausea churning in my stomach.

"They weren't experiencing a psychotic break because of an inability to adapt to human form. It was because of something *we* did to them to prevent them from thinking for themselves."

He looks around the room, turning in his chair as if to ensure we're alone. Then he leans in close, his voice a whisper.

"Don't let him fool you. He's nothing more than a clever dog. He might appeal to your sympathies now, but don't forget who you are, Fatimah Carter. You're my daughter. You're the future head of the Shifter R&D Program. Do what you need to do."

CHAPTER 5

Enforcer

I step up to my door, hesitating to turn the handle as my father's revelations play on a loop in my mind. Chase is standing on the ground, and I can feel his eyes on me even without turning around. He was quiet on the drive home, like he knew I needed some time to process.

I haven't told him what my father said.

I turn, and the afternoon sun seems to have lit a fire in his eyes, making them more golden than brown. He's kind of beautiful.

But his good looks don't excuse the way my body seems to wake up whenever he glances at me, or the way I nearly combusted on the spot when he touched my leg. I've met good-looking men before, even briefly dated a couple of stunners, but I've never reacted this way.

I'm attracted to Chase. I can admit that. He's gorgeous and dangerous. He's kind of sweet and a little mysterious. Of course that combo is going to result in some level of attraction. I can acknowledge that without giving into any crazy, unwelcome fantasies about what it might be like to show him some things he may not know his new body can do...

"Do you want me to leave?"

Yes. The force of that thought takes me by surprise. I want him to leave and go somewhere safe. I don't want him to live and die as an animal the way BioSol's manipulated-

These thoughts are useless.

I am BioSol. Maybe I didn't fully realize the legacy I was trying to live up to, but knowing what my father really did changes nothing. It can't. I've worked too hard to get where I'm at.

My father's right. I know what I need to do.

"Come inside, just for a little while."

The grin that spreads across his face makes my heart hurt, but I turn away and open the door. I need to call and report him. That's my only option if I want to keep my job, my future, my father's legacy.

I thought I needed to fear Chase, but all along it was him who should fear me. I'm the monster.

Once the door's locked behind us, I pull my comm out of my purse. Chase's hands grip my arms with that same searing heat, and I nearly stumble off my feet as he pulls me behind him.

"What the..."

"Who the fuck are you?" Chase's voice is edged with violence, as a man's laughter makes my heart stop. Someone's in my house.

"Easy, friend. I didn't mean to freak you out. I'm just here to talk to Fate."

I recognize that voice.

"Matthew?" I push against Chase's back, trying not to focus on the bunched muscle beneath his shirt as I reassure him there's no danger. "What are you doing here?"

"I'm sorry if I scared you. I'm just making my usual rounds. Checking on our valued employees."

I don't miss the way his eyes dart to Chase, then back to me. And I've never heard of any routine break-ins disguised as safety checkups.

They know.

I start toward the sitting area where the BioSol Enforcer appears to be casually lounging on my sofa, but Chase grips my wrist, keeping me close. He's trying to protect me, and it breaks my heart. I'm not the one who needs to be protected.

I place my hand over his and feel him jerk a little at the contact, but he takes the cue and loosens his grip.

"I'm fine, of course."

Why am I playing dumb? I was going to call, anyway.

Matthew nods, his eyes never leaving mine. "Who's your friend?"

I just need to say the words. Matthew's built like a tank and he's fully armed. If Chase puts up a fight, Matthew will get the upper hand quickly.

This is what I need to do. This is the only option.

Just say the words.

He's a Shifter.

I look back at Chase, expecting to see a hint of anger, defensiveness, or at least wariness. But his expression is relaxed. He looks at me, and a smile plays at the corners of his mouth as he gives me the faintest nod.

He's okay with me turning him in. Moments ago, he was putting himself between me and the perceived danger. Now he's letting me off the hook if I choose to hand him over.

A memory flashes in my mind. A moment that haunted me for years, but I haven't thought about in over a decade. There was a dog; a shepherd mix. When I found him, he was injured, scared, and wildly aggressive. I knew all he needed was love, and someone to show him he didn't need to be afraid. My father took one look at him and no amount of pleading on my part could change his decision. I can still hear the single gunshot that ended that poor soul's chances of ever knowing kindness.

Chase won't survive the night if I go through with this. That's the best-case scenario. After talking with Dad, I'm not so sure that euthanasia will be their first choice. If they're experimenting the way he implied.

I swallow to fight the bile rising in my throat, blinking back the tears stinging my eyes. I'm not that girl anymore, daydreaming about being a vet and saving the world, one sick animal at a time. I'm a lead technician at BioSol, part of the corporation that's turned innocent alien creatures into slaves and uses any means necessary to keep them that way. I kill Shifters. The fact that I didn't know that until now is irrelevant. It's what I do.

But maybe I can save him. Just this Shifter. Just this one time, and maybe no one will ever know.

"This is Chase. He's a friend."

Matthew's eyes narrow, and I look away from his unspoken accusations. How many conversations have we had over the last year about our personal lives? My lack of a social life contrasted with his soul-mate husband and three precocious babies makes for some interesting conversations. If I had a *friend* that looked like Chase, Matthew would already know about him.

But being tempted to try dating again? That's a train wreck he knows I volunteer for every now and then.

"We met this week. It's new, we're just..."

"You're dating?" Matthew's eyebrows shoot through the roof. He must know I'm lying through my teeth. I just saw him two days ago, and if I met someone like Chase, it would have come up.

"Like I said, it's new." I offer a smile that I hope makes me look at ease and not terrified. "I need caffeine. Do either of you want a coffee?"

"I'm good, thanks Fate."

I look back at Chase, and because we're dating, I put a hand on his arm. It's solid as rock and dusted with soft, dark hair. "What about you, babe?"

The endearment comes out a little strangled, but to his credit, Chase doesn't even flinch. Instead, that smile that was playing at the edges of his mouth breaks free to spread across his face. I drop my hand, because touching his skin while being the focus of that much male perfection is going to ruin me.

He reaches up and casually tucks a strand of hair behind my ear. I jump just a little, and I swear I'm on the edge of a flat-out swoon when he trails his fingers along my jaw.

"Sounds good, baby."

Oh fuck.

What have I done?

I babble something that might not be in English and make my way to the kitchen area. Luckily I can make a pot of coffee with my eyes closed, because I can't see straight.

That rolled off his tongue so casually. So naturally. How the heck does he know how to fake date better than I do?

"Are we done here?"

Chase's words jolt me out of my stupor. He hasn't moved, but his focus is on Matthew. The Enforcer raises his hands in mock surrender, standing slowly to his full height, which is nearly a head taller than Chase.

That doesn't deter my fake weekend fling. He walks right up to the bigger man, who puts a hand on the holster of one of his weapons as Chase extends his in an offer to shake. Matthew hesitates for only a moment before accepting the friendly gesture.

"It was good to meet you, man. I'm glad you've got Fate's back. But unless she gives you a key, I don't want to find you in her house uninvited again."

Oh shit, oh shit, oh shit.

"I'm just doing my job."

"Chase, it's okay... really, I-"

"There are other ways to get the intel you need. Be a fucking person."

I can see Matthew brace for this to escalate, but Chase steps off. He strides around the island and takes two coffee mugs off their hooks, setting them in front of the gurgling percolator.

"I'll see you at work, Fate."

"Yeah, for sure."

"If there's anything you need, just shoot me an SOS."

"Thanks, Matthew. I'm good."

He holds my stare, and I know if I so much as blink the wrong way, he'll take the cue.

CHAPTER 6

Want

The door clicks shut, leaving me alone with Chase. My already racing heart doubles its pace. What did I just do? I just lied to Matthew. I lied to BioSol.

I'm harbouring a Shifter who's breaking the law. He's a danger to himself and anyone around him. I could lose my job, my career, my future.

His hand covers mine where I've braced myself on the island, the simple touch sending sparks across my skin. I focus on taking even, calming breaths and the way his long fingers and wide palm dwarf my hand. Prominent veins snake up over his powerful forearm and over the rise of a thick bicep before disappearing under the sleeve of his shirt. Why are men's arms so damn sexy? Is it just me, or do all women melt over a set of strong arms?

"You saved my life."

His words stop my heart. His eyes are too full of emotion. I pull away, needing some distance to think. To breathe. But he cups a hand around the back of my neck and holds me in place as he presses his forehead against mine.

I'm putty in his grasp as his free hand slides up my arm to cup my face. He's still, his hands holding me firmly yet gently. We're breathing the same air and it would take the slightest movement to be kissing his mouth.

"Thank you, Fate. Thank you."

The heat and scent and feel of him draw me in. I want to kiss him. I want to touch his skin and hear his voice when he's so turned on he can't hold back. I lied so he can have a chance at freedom, but I could show him so much more.

The coffee maker sputters its last efforts and goes quiet, and I push away from his grip before my twisted curiosity and inappropriate fantasies override my ability to reason.

"I can't do this. I can't lie again." I retreat until the island is safely between us. "I'm risking everything I've worked for. What you're doing is illegal, and dangerous, maybe, I don't know anymore."

"Why did you lie for me?"

I open my mouth to answer, but I don't know what to say. He doesn't look at me, just casually pours two cups of coffee and raises the first to his lips. I'm mesmerized as he blows steam away from the hot surface before taking the first tentative sip.

His expression is one of wonder as he samples what's likely his first taste of the beverage most humans can't imagine getting through a day without.

What am I going to do?

I take my cup when he holds it out for me, and retreat to the opposite side of the sitting room to stand in front of the wide windows. It's not much of a view. Twenty feet of flat lawn ending at a thin line of trees. The only reason I'm not looking out at a neighbor's house is the little stream that flows on the other side of the tree line. It's not big enough to be considered a river, but it's a protected waterway snaking out from Morwood forest and cutting across town until it meets the ocean.

I've never let anything come between me and my goals. My career is my life. It's not just a job I do, it's who I am. I've got a lot to unpack from what Dad told me, but it doesn't change the fact that I'll do whatever it takes to make a name for myself at BioSol. I won't throw it all away for any man. Or for any creature that worms its way under my skin.

I'll never forget the day I showed Dad my business plans for a little private clinic. His face fell. I'd had the offer from BioSol, and I was going to turn it down, but I couldn't disappoint him. He'd already lost everything to his illness, and I was his last hope to see something accomplished with his legacy.

From the moment you were born, your mother and I knew fate had something big in store for you. This is it. Don't turn your back on it for some childish dream.

I remember his words like the moment was yesterday. And I remember thinking how odd it was that fate, if there were such a thing, would reveal itself to my father and not to me. When I held the offer from BioSol, I certainly didn't feel anything resembling a call from fate.

I feel the heat of his skin before Chase's hand touches my face. He brushes his thumb over my cheek, capturing a tear I hadn't even realized had fallen. I watch as he brings it to his lips, his tongue darting out to lick his thumb.

That might be the sexiest thing I've ever seen.

He takes my hand, bringing it to his mouth to brush his lips against my palm.

"Do you feel this?"

Oh, lord. I can't form words with the way he's holding my hand like it fascinates him, the way he trails his fingers along the inside of my arm from my wrist to my elbow and back. Electricity hums across my nerves as my bones turn to rubber.

I set my coffee down on the window ledge before I drop it.

"When your skin touches mine, it's like...." He presses his lips against my wrist, ensuring I've become nothing more than a puddle of wanting in his grasp. "I can feel it right through me."

He cups a hand behind my neck and I can't breathe as he

releases my wrist and turns his attention to my face, his eyes focusing on my mouth. He leans in, his lips hovering over mine, and I can't think about anything other than what it would feel like to kiss this man.

Because I do feel what he feels. Every touch is electric, every glance from him sends awareness flickering across my skin. Anticipation.

Does he know what he's flirting with right now? Did he absorb that knowledge from his bond with his Agent, or would he be confused if I kissed him? Would it wake up some sexual part of this human body he doesn't even know he possesses?

His mouth brushes against mine. It's the softest contact, yet it nearly brings me to my knees with desire.

I want this. I don't care if he's not quite human, or if it's illegal and morally grey and if I'm caught with him I could lose my-

I stumble backward. Out of his grasp and away from his heat and the smell of his skin, turning away so I can't see the way he's looking at me as his chest rises and falls with heavy breaths.

This is wrong. I can't be attracted to him. Or, I can be... that's just biology at work when he's wearing a body like that. But I can't act on it. I can't encourage him. He's a *Shifter*.

I retrieve my mug of cooling coffee and retreat to the kitchen, taking a calming sip despite my shaking hands. Deep breaths. I'm a grown woman, not a hormonal teenager.

"That can't happen again."

I set my mug on the island and cross my arms before looking back at him. I don't know whether to be pissed off or amused by the almost playful grin on his ridiculously perfect face. He starts toward me, complete confidence in his stride.

I stand my ground. If he thinks that alpha-male crap will work on me...

He stops within arm's reach but doesn't attempt to cross the remaining distance.

"I owe you my life. And if you don't want me to touch you, I swear I won't." He moves closer, as close as he can get without touching, and his voice drops to a sinful rumble. "But I want to."

CHAPTER 7

Indulge

The devil on my shoulder wages war with its angelic counterpart as Chase's statement hangs in the small space between us. But as quickly as he turned up the pressure, he defuses it just as fast with that playful smile that seems to be perpetually hovering just under the surface.

He takes my mug, carrying the matching set to the sink and rinsing them.

"Have you eaten anything today?"

His tone is so casual, it takes my brain a moment to catch up with the shift in the air.

"Um, no. Not yet." I glance at the clock on the stove. It's after two, but I've been so caught up in Chase I haven't even thought about food.

He opens the fridge, contemplating its contents for a moment before pulling out a selection of vegetables. He checks a few cupboards and discovers the pasta, choosing a box of fettuccini noodles to lay out beside the produce. All while I stand and stare, in part trying to process his simple actions, and in part unashamedly appreciating the chance to watch him.

This is okay. I can do this with him; steal these moments and the chance to get to know a little more about him. It's harmless.

"Do you know how to cook?"

He looks up from his inspection of the pasta box and shrugs. "I've never tried."

I guess we're cooking dinner, then.

My heart skips a beat at the idea of doing something so... normal with him. So human. A few more hours won't hurt, right? Whatever Matthew's orders were, or what he suspects, he'll sit on it until Monday at least, considering I gave him no reason to act immediately. He'll respect my privacy, not to mention his desire to avoid getting himself roped into working all weekend.

Chase opens a drawer and pulls out a chopping knife, and I retrieve the cutting board out of its hiding place beside the stove. And just like that, the tension between us is gone. Mostly.

He rinses the veggies while I prep the frying pan and water for the pasta. I watch him chopping like he's been doing it all his life. There's no hesitation in his movements, no awkwardness to indicate that he's never cooked a meal.

"How does it feel to know how to do something, even though you've never done it before?"

"Most of what I know about the world has nothing to do with my own experiences." A muscle twitches his jaw, his brow creasing as he focuses intently on his task.

"You absorbed your Agent's experiences and beliefs when you bonded, and you aged rapidly to match his years. It's part of what makes the Shifter-Human partnership so effective."

"And the removal of free will or the ability to think about my own existence. I'm sure that helps the *partnership* as well."

I don't know how to respond to that. Guilt churns in my gut, but anger soon overshadows it. Anger for what BioSol, for what humans, have done to Shifters.

"They've modified your species to turn you into weapons. Into slaves for our own cause. I believed everything I was told, but now…"

He sets the knife down, glancing at me only briefly before transferring the even slices of bell pepper, onion, and portobello to the sizzling pan.

"Now what do you believe?"

"I believe what I see."

"And what's that?"

I take a deep breath. Acknowledging my rapidly evolving opinion of him feels dangerous somehow. Inviting him to stay, cooking a meal with him like we're old friends or actually on a date; I'm enabling him. But it truly doesn't feel wrong.

"You're not a human, but you're not an animal. There's nothing unnatural about you being in this form. My father said…" I don't know what to believe, really, and I don't want to offer him false hope. But isn't the proof standing right here? "He said it's us who've made it so you can't take this form. It's not that you can't do it. It's that we don't want you to."

He stirs the softening vegetables, his expression unchanging. I force myself to stop staring at his face to try and decode his thoughts, and instead busy myself cleaning up. Soon, the silence feels comfortable, even though I'm still trying in vain to guess what's on his mind.

When the food is ready, he dishes it up and we eat together. It's nice, sharing this with him. I've been so settled into my solitary routine and aside from going out to eat with casual friends or the occasional date, I'm happy to eat alone in my home. But it's nice to have company. Maybe it's just nice to have his company.

We talk about random things, and he asks some questions about my life. Nothing too deep, just nice, light conversation. When we've both eaten our fill, we clean the dishes together.

"Is there any chance we could do this again sometime?"

His question pulls me out of the comfortable, ordinary vibe of the past couple of hours. Can we do this again? What happens now? I open my mouth to reply, but there's so much to consider from that simple statement.

Matthew knew something was off. He wouldn't have been sent here if they didn't at least suspect that I was involved in something. I'm playing house with a Shifter, and BioSol might be plotting to bury us both to hide the evidence.

"It's okay. I didn't mean to put you on the spot."

He cups the back of my head and presses a kiss to my forehead, breaking his promise not to touch me, though I can't say I mind. I close my eyes and focus on the feel of his hand over my hair, and his warm lips on my skin.

"Be safe, Fate. And thank you."

He turns for the door, and a wave of panic washes over me.

"Where will you go?"

He stops and glances back over his shoulder, raising his eyebrows like he's surprised I'm asking. "I can't go back. That's all I know for sure. The rest I'll figure out as I go."

The panic surges, and for a moment I can't reconcile the Shifter in front of me, running to save his life, with the man I just spent the last two hours with. When he walks out that door, will it be minutes, hours, days... how long before they catch him?

"You could stay a little longer."

What am I doing? That is the worst idea I've ever had. He can't stay here. I can't stay anywhere near him, or I'll risk everything I care about.

But I care about him, too. I really wish I didn't. I wish it were just a professional curiosity or misguided attraction. But I care about Chase. I want him to be healthy, and happy, and free.

"I won't put you in more danger than I already have." He clenches his jaw and his fists, and I have the terrifying thought that even if BioSol finds him, they'll have a hell of a fight on their hands.

"They already suspect I'm hiding something. Or at least they're trying to rule out that possibility. If Matthew found any of this suspicious, which I'm sure he would... what do you think he did?"

Chase crosses his arms, his biceps stretching the limits of his shirt. His brow creases as he considers the implications of my words.

"He compared my name with people in the area who match my description. When that came up empty, he called it in. There's likely an Agent waiting to tail me."

"And how long are they going to follow you before they realize their suspicions are true?"

"Not long. I'll head for Morwood, and when I'm close, I'll shift and run. They'll never catch me once I'm in the trees."

He smiles like his plan can't go wrong.

"And then what? Are you planning to live in the forest like an ani-" I catch myself before I say it.

"Like a what?" He uncrosses his arms and walks toward me with confidant strides.

He stops mere inches from me, but I can't bring myself to look him in the eyes.

"You're not an animal. I don't know what I thought before, but you're not an animal."

He's still for a moment, but then lifts his hand to my face. With the lightest touch, he tips my chin and I get a brief glimpse of the emotion in his eyes before he closes them and lowers his face to mine. His lips are full and soft as he presses a kiss to my mouth.

The fleeting connection sparks a flame that spreads through me like a wildfire. Images of us tangled together in the heat of passion flicker through my mind like a kaleidoscope, disjointed and impossible to make sense of. It's more than just attraction. My skin craves his skin, my body's drawn to his like we're already one person.

If I believed in it, this is what fate would feel like. Like the past and the present fusing into this one moment where a single choice can change everything.

"I'd rather live in hiding than go back to the way it was. I won't be anyone's possession. Never again. Living in Morwood, being free to come and go from the cities when I feel like it, that sounds like a damn fine life to me."

"It sounds lonely." I can only whisper the words as I struggle to push my unreasonable, inappropriate, impossible thoughts out of sight and out of mind.

He shrugs like it's no big deal. Like he can't feel the war waging between my body, mind, and heart. Maybe I'm the only one who would feel lonely if he left.

But that's how this has to end. He's not my boyfriend, he's not even my friend. He's a Shifter in human form and he's got two options: run or die for his crime. That's how this has to end. He has to leave and never, ever come back.

But it doesn't have to be tonight.

Once he walks out my door, he's on borrowed time. I won't see him again. I've never been reckless. I've never wasted my time. I've studied, worked, and kept a laser focus on my future.

But Chase is here now. I've already crossed that line by letting him into my home and by lying to cover for him. He's kind, and gentle, and so damn good looking. Why can't I enjoy having him to myself for a little longer? And if he wants to kiss me, would it be so wrong to indulge in that fantasy?

"I want you to stay."

CHAPTER 8

Control

I've never been a damsel in distress. I work hard and make good money. I've got no problem asking a man out to dinner and an evening back at his place when the mood strikes me. Not that I've often met a man tempting enough to warrant that level of effort, but there have been a few.

But Chase. How can he be so damn perfect, and he's not even technically a man?

After he agreed to stay, my sudden raging libido seemed to calm a bit. As if just having him near was enough for now, even though every move he makes tempts my imagination to go where it definitely should not go.

We spent what remained of the afternoon in comfortable conversation. He asked me questions about my childhood, my family, my beliefs, and my dreams. Every answer I gave seemed to fascinate him. It was so easy to tell him everything he wanted to know. Not once did he judge me, or laugh, or suggest my dreams were too small.

Now, as the last of the light fades from the sky and the curtains begin to close, he's cross-legged on the floor, engrossed in my old veterinary textbooks. They were ancient when I bought them, but something about having the physical copies to reference seemed to help my process. He's spent the last hour scouring the pages while I've been curled up on the couch, unable to take my eyes off him for long.

"When did you learn how to read?"

He closes the book and looks up at me, shrugging his shoulders. "I just can."

Something like sadness flickers in his eyes, but he's quick to mask it as he stands up from the floor, gathering the heavy texts and returning them to their place tucked away in a cupboard.

"You would have made a good vet."

A twinge of regret hits me at his words, but I bury it back where it belongs. That ship sailed a long time ago.

"What makes you say that?"

He gives me a sideways look, the grin playing at the corners of his mouth drawing my eyes like moths to a flame. "You're pretty good with animals."

"You haven't..." His meaning registers, and I sit up a little straighter. "You're not..."

His grin widens, and he crouches as his body reforms into the cheetah. But even as he stares at me with those feline eyes, and my heart rate kicks up a notch, there's no denying the honest truth.

"You're not an animal, Chase. You're not entirely human, either. But you're not an animal."

With soundless movements, he lopes across the floor and hops onto the sofa beside me. He's utterly beautiful, and I can't resist the chance to touch him, which starts his chest rumbling with a purr. That sound is something else. There's really nothing like it. I run my fingers through the thick fur at his neck, and he leans into me.

I pet him like an overgrown house cat, and he settles down against my side, his weight heavy against my hip.

We stay like that for a long time. With me tracing the patterns on his fur and him purring impossibly louder as his head lolls against my side. It should be strange that the man I spent the day with is now a cat I'm petting, but in some odd way, it feels perfectly natural.

I'm refusing to imagine what this scene would look like if he were in human form, my hands trailing over his neck, shoulder, and chest. The heat of human skin rather than the softness of fur. It shouldn't make a difference which form he's in, but touching the cheetah feels far less risky than touching the man.

Only now that I'm thinking about it, suddenly this feels dangerously close. The memory of the kiss he gave me fills my mind, and I can still feel the gentle pressure of his mouth on mine. What would have happened if I'd kissed him back?

"I should go to bed. I'm more of a morning person than a night owl." That's the safest option right now. I need to close myself in my bedroom and not think about taking whatever this is to another level.

Energy hums in his body and I move my hand away just as he slips back into human form. It takes my breath away, the sheer impossibility of watching him shift and the sight of the man sitting inches from me, his golden-brown eyes holding mine.

He takes my hand, bringing my palm to his mouth to place a kiss against my skin. Then he presses it against the side of his neck, where I can feel his pulse racing.

"Your touch is the most incredible thing I've ever felt."

He releases his hold on my hand, but I don't immediately pull away. I simply can't. Instead, I trail my fingers down over the smooth skin of his neck as his eyes drift closed. I touch the roughness of the stubble along his jaw. And when I thread my fingers through his hair, his lips part as he sucks in a breath.

Watching the pure pleasure on his face is enough to make me forget every sensible thought I should be having. I push up to my knees and take his face in my hands as I press a kiss to his parted lips.

Doubts and warnings flash in the back of my mind, but I push them away. I want this with him. All of this. I deepen the kiss, finding his tongue with mine and tasting raw desire.

His arms surround me as a growl rumbles in his chest. His hands knead into my back, and he pulls me on top of him until I'm straddling his hips.

This is what I want; what I need. Just for tonight.

I kiss him with a singular focus. Aware only of his mouth, his hands on my back, and the unmistakable ridge of his arousal pressing against my core. He wants this, too, and that knowledge drives me wild with need.

He grips my hips, firmly but gently pushing me off his body.

Embarrassment floods my chest as I realize he's pushing me away, and I break the kiss as I climb off and stumble away from the couch.

What just happened?

When the kitchen island is safely between us, I look back to find him leaning forward, his arms braced on his knees as his chest expands and contracts with breaths as laboured as mine.

What the hell is wrong with me? He's had this body for less than a week. He barely knows who he is, let alone who he wants to be with. And why on earth would I want to be with him? That's the most irresponsible, foolish-

He tilts his head, looking over at me with eyes that slay me.

"I'm so sorry, Chase. That was inappropriate. I shouldn't have taken advantage of you."

He drops his eyes and shakes his head, then stands and walks toward the island as I force my eyes to stay on his instead of dropping to the unmistakable ridge beside the zipper of his jeans.

"Fate. This body's new, but that doesn't mean I don't know what it can do."

The way he says those words sends a shiver down my spine. I nod my understanding and he circles the island, removing the barrier between us. I hold my ground, not entirely sure what's about to happen, but not exactly opposed to any of the options currently racing through my mind.

He stops within arm's reach, his eyes boring into mine as if he can read my thoughts. Part of me wishes he could, because heaven knows the tug-of-war I'm going through makes no sense to me.

"I've seen a lot of shit in my time with Jon. And I know I can hurt you far worse in this form than I ever could with teeth and claws."

I shake my head, because that's one thing I know for certain. "You wouldn't hurt me."

"I felt it. The edge of control. I've seen the other side of that. Females who give up their body willingly because they know the male will take what he wants either way. Sex is a weapon, Fate. And I don't want to use you like that. I can't hurt you."

The gravity of what happened settles on my chest like a physical weight. He didn't push me away because he doesn't want me. He's afraid. Afraid of his own desires because of that asshole who raised him.

"Chase..." I touch my fingertips to his cheek, and his jaw clenches.

"You shouldn't let me touch you again."

"I kissed you. There was nothing non-consensual about that. And you were perfectly gentle."

"I'm not human. You can't want me. And what I'm imagining doing to your body isn't gentle."

I bite my tongue. I know what I should do. I know what I should say. I've always made the right choices; the logical choices. There's no excuse for throwing that logic out of the equation now.

I take a step back, trying to clear my head and form a rational thought. He might technically be a virgin, but he's not naïve. Far from it. But between his Agent and years of catching the scum of humanity, he can't fathom sex that's not rape.

I take a deep breath and step closer to him, my heart pounding in my chest at what I'm about to do. But I want this. With him. No matter what he is or how he got here.

No matter what Monday brings.

I reach out and take his hand, and he lets me raise it to press a kiss to the inside of his wrist.

"Fate." His voice is a warning.

"What if I do want you?"

CHAPTER 9

Worth It

The instant I say the words, heat flares in his eyes. He grips my hips, pressing his forehead against mine as he inhales a deep, slow breath.

"Say it again." His voice is strained and rough at the edges, and I shiver at the thought of what my response will unleash.

I wrap my arms around his neck and brush a kiss across his lips. He doesn't move. I'm not even certain he's breathing. I nip at his lower lip, and his grip on my hips tightens.

"I want you. Now."

His mouth crashes into mine. If I thought our kiss on the sofa was intense, this one is absolutely ravenous.

He grips the top of my thighs, hoisting me as I wrap my legs around his waist. I can tell that he's walking, but this kiss is consuming me. It's all I can focus on. I don't care where he's taking me, what he plans to do with me, or how I'll deal with the consequences of this choice tomorrow.

I want him.

"Are you sure?" His voice is breathless between kisses, but his concern is unnecessary. I've never been more certain of anything. Consequences be damned.

"I'm sure. Don't stop," I practically beg as he lays me on something soft. My bed. And then his mouth is on my skin, doing wicked things down my neck.

"I want you naked."

His voice is barely more than a growl against my skin, yet it's still more question than command. A sliver of nervousness creeps over me, but I help him pull my shirt over my head. My pants are soon thrown against the wall, and my bra and panties follow close behind.

He sits back on his heels. Kneeling between my thighs as his eyes rake over my naked body. I'm on complete display for him.

He puts his hands on my thighs, and heat rages in my body. He slides them up, over my hips, my belly, then he caresses my breasts so gently I want to weep for how desperate I am to have him moving inside me. But he's suddenly not in a hurry.

He explores my body with his hands, his eyes following the path he blazes with such open wonder and amazement that I feel like a goddess. All my flaws and insecurities are meaningless under his inspection.

"You're still dressed."

He pauses as a grin plays at the edges of his otherwise serious expression. Then his bicep flexes as he reaches behind his head and pulls his shirt up and off.

Oh. My. God.

His body is absolute perfection. I want to praise him and tell him how beautiful he is, but I'm literally speechless. My brain has lost its connection with my mouth. All I can do is stare and trace every line and curve with my eyes.

He leans over me, and I welcome his kiss while my hands find the heat of his smooth skin. I explore everything I can touch, but he soon moves from my mouth to trail heated kisses down my neck, over every inch of my chest and my belly, until his lips caress my inner thigh, sending shock waves of desire over my skin and straight to my core.

My hips buck against him. I'm beyond turned on right now. My body is on fire, my heart is racing, and I'm dripping wet. I swear I'm on the edge of an orgasm already, and when he kisses his way back up my body, I'm the one growling.

I slide my hand between my legs, running my fingers over my slick folds and giving my clit the pressure and friction I so desperately need right now. He grabs my wrist and pins it to the bed, then covers me with his mouth. I gasp at the sudden shock of sensation as he sucks and flicks his tongue with expert precision, sending me crashing into an orgasm.

I think I scream. I shamelessly grind my hips against his face, pulling fistfuls of his hair as I hold him in place and ride the endless waves of my climax. I've never come like this. Never knew it was possible.

When I start to come down, and release his head from my death-grip, he slides away. As he stands beside the bed, I can only watch in boneless, post-orgasmic awe as he strips out of his jeans and I get my first glimpse of naked Chase.

He's too much. His body is pure perfection. He climbs over me and as his mouth covers mine, I feel the heavy length of his arousal press against my thigh.

I wrap my legs around his waist, pulling him closer, but he holds back, bracing above me until I meet his searching gaze.

"Are you sure about this... about me?"

"It's all I'm sure about. I want this."

He adjusts his hips and sinks into me, every inch an explosion of sensation that ripples through me, until our hips are flush together.

It feels incredible. He's braced over me, watching my face as I memorize every facet of his expression, his hips still as we simply stare at each other, our bodies joined. I reach up to run my fingers along the ridges of his abs and he brushes a thumb over my cheek.

What is this moment? There should be a name for it, this space between anticipation and the act itself, this moment where we've paused time and I think we could stay here forever, if we choose.

And I would. I would give up anything to stay here in this moment with him. This man who's impossibly beautiful, inside and out. Who's looking at me like there's no one else in the world.

"Fate. You're the most beautiful thing I've ever seen."

The reverence in his voice makes my vision blur. "I was thinking the same thing. I don't want to move."

"I don't want this to end."

I reach up and take his face in my hands. He bucks inside me, and I gasp at the jolt of sensation as a decadent moan falls from his lips. I can't help myself. I want him to make that sound again, so I tighten my legs around his waist and grind my hips against him. He throws his head back, pure pleasure consuming his expression as he matches my movements, then grips my hips and takes over to pull out and thrust into me in a steady, building pace.

Now I'm the one moaning. The feel of him moving inside me is beyond comprehension. I can't think, I can only feel.

"Are you okay?"

His concern for my comfort makes my heart hurt. His arms are braced and shaking. His abs are tight. He's holding back.

"It feels amazing. You're amazing. Please, don't hold back." I can hear the breathless desperation in my voice, and he doesn't hesitate to grant me my request.

He hooks my leg and pushes it high, gaining a better angle as he braces his other arm above my shoulder to anchor me. And then he lets himself go. All I can do is hold on and make sure he knows how incredible this is with a steady stream of *fuck yes, don't stop*, and whatever other two-word phrases my brain can manage while I'm being fucked beyond my wildest dreams by this man I shouldn't want. By this Shifter I shouldn't have.

My orgasm comes all too soon. I don't want this to end. But he's right there with me and his roar of pleasure sends my climax through the roof. He thrusts into me even harder before burying himself one last time and going still.

He drops my leg. His face is in my neck, and I'm pretty sure he bit me. That thought makes me laugh, but he's still trying to catch his breath and when he lifts to look at me with a curious expression, I grip his face and kiss him lazily.

"That was... wow."

I feel him smile against my mouth. He carefully pulls out of my body, then settles down at my side, pulling me close. "Are you sure I didn't hurt you?"

His hand traces my body as his eyes hold mine, concern etching his forehead.

"If I'm sore in the morning, it'll be so worth it."

His smile lights up the room and pain slices through my chest. I push it down and focus on him; on this gorgeous, perfect, naked man in my arms. I won't let thoughts of what comes next mar this incredible memory.

CHAPTER 10

Enough

"Clearly I'm no expert, but this is fucking brilliant"

I shake my head, waving off his statement like it's no big deal. But even with a mouthful of rocky road ice cream, I can't hide my grin at his praise.

"I'm serious, baby." He sets my decade-old business plan down on the island, smoothing the faded paper with an almost reverent touch. "The comparisons you've outlined between a typical clinic and your vision for it are beautiful. I seriously love it."

He leans toward me, and I take the cue to offer a spoonful of the decadent treat. I could honestly watch this man eat ice cream all day, wearing nothing but a light pair of sweat pants, which he conceded to wear only when it became clear we'd never keep our hands off each other long enough to eat if we didn't give in and put clothes on.

Heaven help me, this day has been something out of a dream.

He pushes the bowl away and hooks an arm around my waist, pulling me against his warm, solid body. He holds me tight as I wrap my arms around his waist, and I know his thoughts have drifted to the same place as mine. To the realization that a night of passion, a day of half-dressed, dopey conversation, a weekend of getting to know each other in every way possible... it's all we have. And it's not enough.

He dips down and scoops an arm behind my thighs, lifting me off the ground as I squeal and grip his neck for dear life. He carries me to the sofa, the early afternoon sun bathing the space in warm light as he settles into the cushions with me cradled on his lap.

I trace the lines of his shoulder, his collarbone, his chest. His skin is my obsession. I can't get enough of the feel and taste of him.

I adore this man, and I love who I am with him. I don't remember the last time I felt this connected to a single moment in time, or this comfortable in my own skin, or this cherished.

"Are you happy?"

I meet his gaze as I consider his loaded question. Am I happy? What does that even mean to me?

"In this moment, yes."

He shakes his head. "No, I mean with your life."

He adjusts our positions so he can better look into my eyes, and I know he's not looking for a simple answer. If it were anyone else asking such a thing, it would be an easy yes. Accomplished, motivated, driven, enthusiastic... all strong words that I've defined myself with. But when's the last time I slowed down and simply existed in a moment? Have I ever had a day like this, where my only desire is to just be still and appreciate what I have right now?

"Happiness is too simple a concept. It sounds lovely on the surface, to strive to be happy. But the reality is that to accomplish anything in life it's not about being happy, it's about focus and hard work. Those are the only things that will mean anything in the end."

He brushes my hair back from my face, then cups my cheek to draw me in for a slow kiss. I nip at his bottom lip, feeling his cock buck against my thigh in response. I can't resist slipping a hand under the waist of his pants, gripping him tightly as he hardens fully within my grasp.

I stroke him lazily as we kiss, and he slides his hand up my thigh to cup my sex, petting me with unhurried movements until I'm grinding against his hand, desperate for more friction. He grips my thighs, maneuvering me with ease until I'm straddling his hips and sinking down onto his body.

He fills me so completely. Not just physically, as his body stretches mine in the most wonderful way, but it's my heart that feels full beyond measure. Every look, touch, and word from him just... it's beyond anything I knew could exist between two people.

"I don't think it's that complicated."

It's a struggle to stay still and enjoy this moment, when my body's desperate to move against his and take the pleasure that's so close. But I love that he loves this in-between place as much as I do.

"What do you mean?"

"Happiness." He tips my chin up and I open my eyes. His are dark with desire, and I know he's fighting as hard as I am to remain unmoving. "I think this is it, right here. All the rest is just optional."

I smile and kiss his lips. "Sex is happiness? I think right now I might agree with you."

He shakes his head, gripping my hips to keep me still when I try to writhe against him. "No, not just that. Us. Having someone who sees only you. Who wants you without condition or judgement. Sharing our bodies, our dreams, our future. Loving someone and being loved just as hard in return."

I blink back the sudden emotion I feel at his words. "Chase, I..."

"It's okay, baby. I know we can't have all of that." He kisses my forehead, then pulls me down so I'm tight against his body, my ear against his racing heart as I'm wrapped in his arms. "But I can imagine what it would feel like with you. If I could keep you."

Tears threaten, but I won't cry today. We both know this is our beginning and our end all wrapped together, and I won't mar the memories with sadness. I move my hips, and he takes the cue. Even though he'd softened slightly as we spoke, he's back to full strength in moments and our movements quickly escalate from gentle lovemaking to an orgasm-chasing frenzy.

I love being on top with him. Setting the pace, watching his expressions as I take the lead for his pleasure and my own. He's impossibly powerful, a deadly predator when he chooses to be, and it drives me simply wild to watch him as he submits himself beneath me.

When I come apart it only slows us for a moment before he flips me around and takes the top, bringing me to the edge again in mere minutes. He's gotten too good at holding his own climax at bay, swapping our positions and holding me in place when I've become boneless from too many orgasms to count. And when he finally lets himself go, it's a spectacular thing to witness.

"I love you."

His words stop my heart as I'm losing my battle with consciousness, wrapped in his heat on the sofa in an incredible after-sex glow. The admission should scare me, but I pull his hand up to my face and nuzzle into his wide palm.

Maybe he's right. Maybe happiness could be enough.

CHAPTER 11

Monday

I like to stretch out when I sleep. The idea of sharing the precious real estate of my mattress or, gasp, my blankets, has always sounded absolutely appalling.

I stand corrected.

Waking up to strong arms around me, a warm hand on my hip, and a firm, naked body moulded against mine... that's a little bit of paradise. I turn slowly, just enough to really drink him in. With the hard lines of his body softened in sleep, he's utterly stunning.

Oh fuck.

Reality hits me like a kick in the sternum.

It's Monday. I didn't set my alarm.

I scramble out of bed as he wakes up with a jolt, the red nine-something a blur on my clock.

"You okay?" His voice is thick with sleep, and even though a tiny part of me is coaxing to call in sick and savor some dopey morning sex, I don't look back.

I've never been late for work.

I shoot off a short text and race through an even shorter shower, then throw on clothes while ignoring the naked vision of a man watching my every move.

I mumble an apology, though I'm not sure what I'm apologizing for. I'm only sorry for being careless and letting my responsibilities take a back seat to a moment of pleasure.

An arm loops around my waist as I hurry for the door, and I can't help but melt as he pulls me tight against him and nuzzles into my neck, his impossibly talented mouth finding that spot that makes me weak in the knees.

Did this weekend really happen?

"Stay." His voice is husky and full of dirty promises. Promises I know he's willing and able to deliver. He backs me against the island and makes certain I can feel how ready he is.

Heaven help me, I lost count. Lost count of the orgasms, of the kisses, of the whispered *what ifs*. And I lost track of time. Of reality. Of all those things his touch makes me want to forfeit in exchange for one more moment of everything he makes me feel.

"Chase, stop."

Even I can hear the edge of arousal in my voice, the need drowning out the words themselves. But as much as ending this is going to hurt, it's the only way this was going to go. The pain of losing what I never really had is the least I deserve for what we've stolen.

He releases his grip on my hips, bracing himself on the edge of the island and caging me in the circle of his arms.

"I'm not ready to let you go."

A part of me melts at his words, but I grit my teeth and latch on to a more useful emotion. Anger. Anger at the world for not seeing how human he is. Anger at myself for letting my heart get tangled up in this forbidden tryst.

"I don't have time for this." His eyes snap to mine and I can see the sting of my words. But this is how it needs to be. It won't do him or me any good for me to let him see how close I am to falling. "A weekend fling is one thing, but I can't have this spilling over into my work week. I can't fuck up everything I'm working for just to..."

He steps back, avoiding eye contact. I swallow the words my heart needs him to hear as I grip the edge of the island with white knuckles to keep from reaching for him.

"Don't be mad. This was fun. It was amazing. But work is my priority."

"I guess that's one human trait I'll never understand."

"I'm sure it's nice not to have such *human* obligations."

Something sparks in his eyes, but I don't have time to feel guilty or give in to the emotions at war inside me. I'm late for work after risking everything to get closer to him. If I lose my job; If they learn what I've done...

I can't think about that now. I grab my keys and pull the door open. But my feet don't take the hint.

I'm late. And judging by the morning traffic on my sleepy street, the highway's going to be packed and I'll be lucky to make it to my office by late morning.

But I can't bring myself to step through the door.

Against my better judgement, I look back over my shoulder. He's standing where I left him. Naked and perfect with his arms crossed and an expression that holds none of the joy and pleasure of last night.

"It's okay, Fate. I'm good. We both knew today was coming."

That stabbing pain hits me square in the chest once again. I really wish it was a heart attack, or maybe lung cancer. Something serious, but curable. But even though I've never felt this before, I know what it is as surely as I know how to breathe. Despite all the reasons I shouldn't, I've fallen in love with him.

It doesn't make sense. It's illogical and dangerous. Even if we were the same species, I still barely know him.

But here we are.

The door clicks shut, and he welcomes me into his arms. I slide my hands over his skin, unable to resist touching him. He hardens instantly, but tips my chin for a soft, unhurried kiss.

"Thank you," he whispers against my lips.

"I wish-"

He stops my words with another kiss, this one deep and demanding and all too brief.

"There's no place for me in your life. I know that."

"Chase..."

He pins me with a stare that makes me bite my tongue.

"I love you. I'll keep that feeling and the memories you gave me for as long as I live. I love you for who you are; strong, independent, dedicated, and passionate. But I also love you for who you've helped me become."

I blink back my tears. "Who are you?"

He swipes his thumb across my cheek, and damn if that playful hint of a grin doesn't make my body light up.

"Whoever I want to be."

I can't stop my smile, because that answer is everything. Less than a week ago, he was at my door with no idea how he fit into the world. Now, he has his whole life in front of him.

"You need to go far away from here. Don't take any chances." I blink back fresh tears, kissing his skin and memorizing the feel of him in my arms. "But I wish you could stay."

It's the truth, and that terrifies me. I want to keep him. I want to keep us.

"I can't deny there's part of me that would have me begging at your feet for the chance to exist solely as your house cat and slave to your sexual desires..."

The image he paints isn't at all unappealing, and I laugh as I trail my fingers across his skin. I can't ignore the third presence in this conversation any longer, but when I grip the hard, thick length of him he growls and grabs my wrists, bringing my arms up and around his neck.

"If you start that, there's no way you're getting to work anytime soon."

He kisses me, and I nip at this lower lip. "You started it when you opted out of clothing."

He pulls me tight against him as his kiss moves to my neck. Soft lips, coarse stubble, and the bite of teeth drive me mad with desire. But then he stops. His forehead presses to mine as he takes deep breaths.

"I'm sorry. You need to go to work."

"I wish I could call in sick..."

"If you do, I'm going to fuck you right here."

Oh lord. I want that so badly.

"Will you be here when I get back?"

"If that's what you want. I'll take every moment you choose to give."

Accusation

"Good…" Matthew exaggerates the effort of looking at the huge, digital clock imbedded in the wall behind reception. "Morning?"

I give him a glare that says 'you don't want to pick a fight with me right now', and he raises his hands in mock surrender. The receptionist offers her usual canned greeting as I swipe my comm and push through the heavy double doors leading to the labs. I can feel Matthew's eyes follow me as I hurry to my wing.

He walks pretty soundlessly for a big man.

"How's the new boyfriend?"

I take some calming breaths as I turn on the various equipment I'll need throughout the day, starting with the coffee maker. My current least-favorite lab tech is out again, so I'm not only behind on my own Monday tasks, but now I'm behind on hers, too. It's the last straw. There are plenty of eager techs looking for work in the field. I don't need to entertain someone who's less than committed to her career.

"Fine. He's fine, we're fine. No babysitting required."

"Seems a little sudden, is all."

I finish signing into the system and retrieve my favorite coffee mug to swipe the first cup of the morning. With my day officially started and my calendar mercilessly declaring that I've got ten minutes to spare before my first appointment, I settle into the worn desk chair and give the suspicious Enforcer my full attention.

"It's not sudden, Matthew. I'm twenty-eight years old and this is the first time I've had a sleepover with a boy in my own home. That's not sudden, that's pathetic."

He cracks a smile and shakes his head, which should probably bring the tension down a notch. But I'm still wound tight from the weekend, from the intensity of our goodbye this morning, and just from the emotional shit I've got to sort through with all of this. The drive to work was not enough. I need time to think.

"You've never been late for work before."

"I know. And it won't happen again."

"Hey, no judgement from me. I'm just worried about you."

The first biting sip of java and a few deep breaths calm my nerves enough that I don't bite his head off for giving a shit.

"There's nothing to worry about. You saw the man. Tell me you'd get to work on time if you woke up next to that in your bed."

He doesn't say a word, just strides across the room to hold out a fist for knocking.

"Exactly." I can't help but laugh, even though that's not exactly the way things played out this morning.

There was no morning sex, just a whole lot of me being pissed off. I didn't need to be bitchy. It wasn't his fault I forgot to set my alarm. And then he turned it all around by being impossibly sweet and sexy, and damn... if I'd called in sick...

But these thoughts and feelings are just further proof of how much I've messed this up. I can't keep playing house with a Shifter. The weekend was fun, but it's Monday now. If he's still there when I get home, we need to end this for real. He needs to go somewhere safe.

"I'll see you at lunch?"

Matthew's still looking at me like I'm a safety hazard, and I give him what I hope is a reassuring smile.

"Yeah. That would be nice." At least I can relax a little now, knowing he didn't report me or Chase, or send another Agent to watch my house. He wouldn't be this playful if he had. Matthew's an honest person and a terrible liar when he tries.

He leaves to make his rounds or stand at the door looking intimidating, and a moment later my first appointment of the day arrives.

It's a wolf Shifter with a malfunctioning Link implant. He'll need it replaced, but first I do a full evaluation to ensure he's fit for the surgery, which he is. His Agent's a tattooed hulk of a man with a permanent scowl, but his eyes are misty as he tells me it's been nearly a week since he's been able to talk to his Shifter through their implant.

The two of them clearly share a bond that goes well beyond what's necessary for their partnership to work. He cares about his furry counterpart, and judging by the wolf's body language, the feeling's mutual.

The four other teams I meet throughout the day are as varied as they come, though most of my time is filled with the usual Monday backlog of tests leftover from the weekend. It's busy enough that I don't have time to meet with Matthew for lunch, and I definitely don't have time to think about what's going to happen when I get home from work.

A heavy knock signals my last appointment of the day, though I can't find any paperwork to indicate who it is or what they're here for. Until a familiar voice says my name.

An icy chill crawls up my spine as I meet Agent Bates' eyes.

He stands in my doorway, an expectant look on his face. I glance past him, into the hallway, as if I'm expecting to see a Shifter at his heels.

"Agent Bates, hello. Where's your partner today?"

He smirks, then closes the door behind himself. He picks up a chair and places it in front of mine, taking a seat so we're eye to eye. "My cat hasn't been right since he met you."

I try to channel my panic into a look of confusion, but he's staring at my every movement. Assessing my reaction.

"What are you implying, exactly?"

"What did you say to him?"

"Nothing, I..."

He narrows his eyes, his jaw clenching.

"I see a lot of Shifters. I don't recall your particular-"

"He wasn't himself after we left here last week. He disappeared for a night, then came home, but now he's been gone for four days."

"I'm sorry, Agent, but I assure you it has nothing to do with me." I cross my arms, then uncross them and grab my tablet, trying not to shake as I retrieve his file and my notes from our first visit. "Wasn't he acting strange? That's why you brought him in, if I remember correctly?"

I find the file and hand the tablet over. I've got nothing to hide, other than the man I just slept with is actually his Shifter in human form. But nothing here will point to that.

"Potentially abusive?" Bates looks up from the tablet with emotionless eyes.

"Those were my observations based on what I witnessed. They're meant for internal use only, so I apologize if reading them makes you uncomfortable. I never intended for you to see that."

"It's none of your fucking concern how I treat my Shifter."

"Which is why my observations are just that; observations. The relationships between Agents and their bonded Shifters interest me, so I make notes. I mean no disrespect."

He sets the tablet down onto my desk hard enough that I'll be surprised if the screen isn't cracked.

"Did you feel bad for him? Did you talk to him?"

"Of course not."

"And if he came crawling to you for more..." He very

deliberately scans my body with his eyes. "Sympathy. Would you help him hide?"

"I know you're worried about your partner, so I won't take offence to what you're implying. But BioSol already sent an Enforcer to break into my house and check up on me. I'm assuming that was related to this." I cross my arms to keep from squirming under his intense stare.

His chair squeals across the floor as he stands abruptly, and I do the same. Not that it keeps us anywhere near an even playing field, since he's a wall of muscle and weaponry.

He steps in closer, but I resist the urge to take a step back. His nose is practically touching mine as he slides a hand around my neck.

"You're hiding something. When I find out what it is…"

The hand around my neck tightens, but I refuse to react. He's trying to intimidate me. He's not going to murder me at BioSol.

"Maybe I won't turn you in. Maybe I'll keep the evidence to myself, and you and I can work out a more private arrangement."

Bile rises in my throat. This asshole is the reason Chase didn't think sex could be consensual.

"There's no evidence, because I've done nothing wrong. And I'd happily go to prison before I'd let you blackmail me into being raped, you sick fuck."

He squeezes my neck hard enough that an involuntary whimper escapes, and the smile that spreads across his face makes it clear he likes that sound a little too much. He drops his hand and steps back, returning the chair to its rightful place and walking out of my office without another word or glance.

CHAPTER 13

Burdens

"It's unnatural. Disgusting."

Dad's voice trails off into mumblings, and I stand up to peer through the curtains for the countless time. I parked on the street so I can keep an eye on my car. I can't shake the feeling that someone's watching me, even now.

Take a week off. You deserve it. Yeah, right. My boss's words seemed almost caring, until I tried to decline my so-called vacation and he made it abundantly clear it wasn't a suggestion. *An Agent suspecting a BioSol employee of tampering with their Shifter isn't good for our image or yours. Take a week while the situation's being resolved.*

I've never taken a week off. Hell, I've never taken a day off.

What have I done?

Dad's silent, and I watch his face in the fading light from the window. He looks almost peaceful now, but his eyes are unfocused, and I can see the tight grip he has on the arm of his chair.

I smooth his thinning hair and kiss the top of his head. I don't know why I came here today. My father's legacy wasn't what I thought it was. All I've wanted is to carry on where he could not, but after learning BioSol's true motives, I can't stomach the idea of being part of that.

Is Chase unique? Are all Shifters capable of taking human form; of thinking and feeling and loving like we do? It's unfathomable that we've taken an entire species and moulded them into weapons. Into slaves.

I don't know if I can do it. Any of it. I just want to go back to last week. Last Monday, when I had a full workweek ahead and no complications.

"Hello, Fate."

I jump at the nurse's cheery greeting, and she giggles. "I'm sorry, love, you were lost in your own little world there!"

"Yes, I..." I look over at Dad, and he's looking back at me.

She pats my shoulder. "He's doing well today, aren't you Cliff? Had a great weekend, too."

"That man of hers isn't a man. He's an animal. It's disgusting. Filthy."

I feel the heat in my cheeks as I mumble an apology to Peggy and grab my purse on my way out the door.

"Fate!"

I stop in the hallway as she catches up.

"I know it's hard, but try not to let that kind of talk get to you. He's just worried about you, and his mind embellishes."

I shake my head. "Maybe he's right."

She chuckles and mocks a fanning motion. "Well, love, I saw the man you came in with over the weekend. Even if he howls at the full moon, I think it would take more than that to make him qualify as disgusting."

I can't help but laugh at that. And how right she is. No woman in her right mind would turn a man like Chase away. Yet, that's exactly what I need to do. Maybe that's why I came here, to delay getting home and having to end this. Maybe I'm hoping if I'm late enough, he'll already be gone. That would be easiest for both of us.

"If you don't mind me saying," Peggy leans in close, her voice dropping, "You work too much. And I'd venture to say it's partly because of that man." She points back toward dad's door. "Now, Cliff's a good patient. And I love all the souls in my care. I want the last chapters of their lives to be as pleasant as possible, regardless of how they lived before they came here.

But you don't need to live your life to please your father. If you spend your days worrying over making him happy, you're going to end up exactly where he is; bitter at the world and putting your burdens on your children's shoulders."

I shake my head and blink back the stinging tears. She makes it sound so simple, but I can't just walk away from everything I've worked for my entire adult life.

Peggy puts a hand on my arm, "It's okay for happiness to be your priority, even if that doesn't seem to match the world's definition of success."

CHAPTER 14

Trust Me

"We can't do this."

I turn my back at the way Chase's face falls. How did he think this was going to end? He's a Shifter. I'm a human. It's not like happily ever after was in the cards.

Peggy's advice was nice to cling to for a moment, but it's not how the real world works. When I walked in the house and found him still here, it felt so right to fall into his arms and forget everything but the way I feel when I'm with him.

But we can't do this.

He pulls me tight against the solid wall of his chest. I want to push him away and melt into his embrace. I want to scream at him to leave me alone, and I want to kiss him until we're one person.

"It's okay, Fate." His mouth brushes my neck, then the soft bite of teeth. "It would have been easier if I'd left before you came home, but I couldn't bear not seeing you again. You've given me a new life. You've shown me what love feels like. I'll be forever grateful."

I swallow the lump in my throat, blinking back the tears that threaten to slip out along with all the words I can't ever say to him. I love you. I need you.

Stay.

I bite my tongue to keep from making this harder than it already is.

He tips my chin and his mouth covers mine in a soft, deep kiss that I'll commit to memory, along with every other touch, taste, and sound from these moments with him.

As if he knows my heart can't handle any more, he steps back and turns for the door. And just like that, he's gone. I know without a doubt that I'll never see him again. Not because he doesn't care, but because he cares enough to respect my wishes.

Knowing that makes this a million times harder. How often in one lifetime do you find someone that perfect? Never, I suspect.

But I'm wallowing. What's done is done. I need to appreciate that I had an amazing weekend and made some memories to keep me warm for a long, long time. With one final whispered wish for his safety, I turn for the kitchen.

Wine, carbs, and the replay of that genetic engineering conference I missed last week. That's what I need now.

With glass in hand and nachos cooling on the coffee table, I scroll my comm for the first lecture. I'll use my week off to up level my knowledge, and I'll return on Monday even stronger. A clear purpose and a plan to forget what could have been, if the world weren't so cruel.

Nevermind the flicker of doubt that threatens my resolution, or the slight nausea that settles in my gut at the idea of spending my life as one of the faces of BioSol; the company who enslaves Shifters.

I shake my head and take a long sip, debating between two equally fascinating topics when there's a soft knock at my door. I nearly drop my comm.

"Fate?"

I take a deep breath and another long sip of wine. His voice is muffled through the door, but it's him. He came back. Why would he do that? Was one goodbye not hard enough? I set my glass down before my shaking hands can spill the crimson liquid.

I contemplate not going to the door at all. But the thought of seeing his face one more time. Kissing him one more time...

I should not open that door. I can't say goodbye to him twice.

As seems to be the pattern where he's concerned, my body doesn't care what my brain is telling it. My hand's turning the door handle before I can think about all the reasons why this is a terrible idea.

I pull it open and my heart stops.

"Agent Bates?"

The smile that spreads across his face sends an icy chill across my skin.

"Hello, Fate. How's our cat tonight?"

"I told you already, I..."

He makes a chastising noise with his tongue as he shakes his head. "You've had your chance to lie to me, sweet thing. I'm not here to ask more questions."

He steps forward and I don't think, I just shove the door closed. But instead of a satisfying slam in his cocky face, there's just the dull thud of wood hitting muscle as his fingers curl around the frame. I don't waste time trying to question his motives or get past him. I just bolt for my bedroom.

I can lock myself in and call for help. If needed, the window there is big enough for me to crawl out of.

I get to the open doorway when something heavy hits me between the shoulder blades, forcing the air from my lungs and propelling me forward until I'm sprawling across my bed.

I don't scream. There's no one to hear me, anyway. I just scramble to get my legs under me and keep moving and breathe as I fumble with my comm. I need to call the-

My comm's ripped from my grasp as hands grip my arms and flip me onto my back. I kick and punch and bite, but it takes him seconds to immobilize me with his weight straddling my hips, my wrists locked in one of his gigantic hands, and his free hand gripping my jaw hard enough to make me taste my own blood.

I'm completely helpless in his grasp. Forcing my body not to struggle and my mind not to panic is a nearly impossible feat. But neither will help me now.

He leans down until his face is close to mine. I can smell that he's been drinking.

"I know you sheltered him."

I try to shake my head, to deny the accusation, but the hand on my face makes it impossible.

"I want to know everything he said. Everything he did. Do you hear me?"

I attempt a nod. He knows what Chase can do. It's not just a hunch, he knows.

"If you hit me, I will break your hand. If you try to bite me or scream, I will knock you the fuck out and we can try again when you wake up. Understand?"

I don't try to nod this time. I just close my eyes.

He laughs, as if he's amused by my willingness to deescalate this. Like there'd be any logic in thinking I can gain any amount of physical upper ground here.

"Good girl."

His weight doubles, his chest crushing against mine before his body flies backward and a primal roar tears from his lungs. All I can see is a blur of spotted fur as I scramble to the far side of my bed and onto my feet.

Chase is in cheetah form.

He's got Agent Bates pinned on his back and they're staring each other down. I can guess by the intent expressions that they're talking through their link.

Chase will reason with him. He'll explain everything. There's no way Agent Bates can deny the man Chase clearly is.

He shifts, and Bates' eyes go wide.

"Trust me," Chase says, rising to his feet and holding out a hand to help him off the floor. A peace offering.

As much as I hate that asshole, the fact that Chase is willing to extend an olive branch makes my chest swell with pride. He's a good man, semantics be damned.

Agent Bates moves impossibly fast as he pulls a gun from the holster on his hip. I scream his name, but Chase melts back into cheetah form and locks his jaws on Bates' neck.

The gun goes off as a bone-chilling roar is torn from Chase, and I instinctively drop to the floor. The silence after the explosion of sound is deafening, but I can't bring myself to peer over the top of the bed.

He shouldn't have been here. He should have left this place far behind.

A moment later, arms loop around my waist and lift me off the floor.

CHAPTER 15

Plan

It's over. Everything I worked for. Everything I thought my life would be.

"I'm so sorry. I'll fix this."

I stop pacing the floor, turning on my heels as anger boils in my veins.

"You can't fix this. You-"

The look on Chase's face takes the fight out of me. His eyes are so full of sorrow, it's painful to meet his gaze.

He killed his Agent. Holy Shit.

I've been terrified and fuming over the consequences of this whole mess. Of how I can explain what happened to keep my job, my freedom, my life. But Chase...

Shifters can't survive without their bondmates. When that connection is severed, the Shifter wastes away and dies. For the first time since this whole mess started, my vision blurs and I can't stop the tears that escape. I try to turn away, but Chase scoops me into his arms and kisses my face.

"Don't be scared. I'll fix this. I swear." He holds me tight, comforting me like I'm the one with the most to lose. "You'll lock yourself in the bathroom and call the Protectors. Tell them I attacked you. Jon tried to stop me." He presses my comm into my hands. "They'll believe you. You won't be blamed for any of this, I swear."

He swipes a tear from my face, kisses my head, and turns away.

It's really that simple. Chase is already in the system as having potential behaviour issues, after Bates brought him in to get assessed. And I'm off work because of his accusations, so if Bates showed up at my house to pursue it and his Shifter snapped...

I slide my comm into my back pocket.

"Chase, wait."

He stops but doesn't look back.

I've always thought of myself as an intelligent woman. I value continuous learning and hard work, and there's never been a point in my life where I've doubted my ability to reach my goals.

But I've spent my entire adult life putting all that energy into someone else's dreams. I wanted to make my father happy, but his legacy is one of suffering and servitude for an entire species. If I turn my back on this man who cares about me and who I could truly love, that will make my father happy. If I turn him in to face his fate with BioSol, that will be in line with my father's so-called legacy.

He's going to die, either way.

I grip the back of the sofa, my legs suddenly unable to hold me steady on their own. "Your bondmate..."

His eyes narrow as if he's not sure what I'm implying. Then his expression softens, and he closes the distance to take my face in his hands. His lips part like he's about to say something, but instead he pulls me into his arms, crushing me against his body in a tight hug. And I'm right there with him, my arms around him as I hold on like I might never let go.

"My bond with him is broken."

"I know." Fresh tears spill down my cheeks, but Chase only holds me tighter.

"It was broken before this. I could feel it. Our connection just... faded."

I jolt backward, searching his face for some sign he's only making this up to help me feel better.

"Are you serious?"

His smile melts me. And now my thoughts are racing as I thread this new information into what I thought the future looked like. Chase can survive. He can have a life and a future.

"You need to go. You need to get far away from here."

He pulls me in for another hug and kisses the side of my head. I feel his hands slide down my back, and he slips the comm out of my pocket. Pressing it into my hands once again, he tilts my head so I'm looking him square in the eyes.

"You need to call."

"No, Chase. I'm not doing that. I can't do that..."

"There's no other option. You're not losing your job for me, or worse."

I push away from him, turning my back because I can't look at him and picture the outcome of what he's telling me to do. This can't be the only way. This can't be how it ends, not when he finally has a future to call his own.

"Now, Fate. Lock yourself in the bathroom and make the call."

His voice is a command, and my feet obey. I walk toward my bathroom, then stop in my tracks at the start of the short hallway. He's there. I can only see his legs, if I don't go any further. He's just lying there on the floor.

Chase killed a man. He murdered an Agent. *His* Agent.

I turn around, and Chase is in cheetah form. Perched on the couch like an overgrown house cat. His face is a mask of calm, only the tip of his long tail twitching to give away his agitation.

There's a dead body in my house.

And there's a man who loves me.

Maybe he's not quite human, but he's more of a man than any I've met. And the way he loves me is so raw, so pure, so intense. It's not just the amazing sex, though that's definitely a perk. It's the moments in between. The way he cares for me, touches me, gives me space when I need it and seems to instinctively know when I need him close.

But can I really claim to know his heart after so few hours together? What does it say about my own sanity that I'm considering giving up everything I care about for him?

My father would...

Chase turns his head and meets my eyes. He just holds my gaze, and even in cat form I feel the way he sees me. Really sees me, with no judgement and no expectations.

My father's legacy was ensuring Shifters stay in their place. That their true nature as independent people never be discovered. No one knows what they really are. Even Shifters themselves don't know what they're capable of.

It's a business, plain and simple. We profit from these creatures we've purchased and turned into living weapons. I don't want to be part of that. I don't want my name on any piece of BioSol. Even if there's no future for Chase and me, that's a decision I'm making for myself. Not for him, or my father, or some ridiculous notion of self-importance.

"I love you, Chase."

His body tenses, his pupils blowing wide. But he doesn't move from his place. He won't do anything that will put me in more danger. He would never do that.

"What if I don't want my job back? What if I don't want my life back? What if you've shown me who I am, and I'm not the person I thought I was? What if I can't imagine a future without you in it?"

I swipe the fresh tears. I've never been a crier. Never been quick to get emotional over stuff I can't control. My father said that was because I was strong, but maybe it was because I never had to think about what came next. The path was laid out for me, and regardless of how I felt, time would move forward and I would do what needed to be done to please my father, my teachers, my boss.

His arms surround me and I wrap mine around his waist. I cling to him, knowing that this moment is stolen and every moment that I get to spend with him will be just as fragile.

"You are my life, Fate. Everything I am is yours. That's been true since the moment you touched me and told me I could be more. You've given me a lifetime of love in the short time we've had together."

"We can't let this go. We need a plan."

CHAPTER 16

Time

"And you didn't notice anything unusual before the attack?"

"I've told you all the exact same thing." I take a deep, calming breath. "I'm sorry, I don't mean to sound frustrated."

"It's fine. Take your time. It's been a long night."

I try to muster a smile for the man, but it quickly dies.

"Agent Bates had concerns, but nothing I saw indicated that his Shifter was violent. He was calm... until he wasn't. It just happened so fast..."

I let my voice trail off, hoping he'll be satisfied with the answer.

I've been nothing but cooperative, if a little distant. Everything that happened with Bates. My conversations with Chase. Watching him walk out the door, not knowing for sure if I'll see him again. It's all left me feeling like I'm walking in someone else's body. Someone else's life.

First, they questioned me in my living room. Then a sparse office at the Protector's headquarters. Now, I'm in a comfortable room with a view at BioSol where they're more interested in the 'rogue' Shifter than they are in the Agent who died.

"I'm sure they'll find him. If they don't, nature will take its course and he won't be a danger for much longer."

I refuse to focus on that statement, and the reminder that Chase was never meant to survive his Agent's death. I look up at the abstract clock on the wall. It's five a.m. and at this point, no amount of coffee is going to stop me from taking a nap in the very near future.

There's a tidy white desk that sits in front of a wide window. The name on the door said 'Marilyn', but I haven't spoken with a woman tonight.

"What's your name?" I ask, fighting back a yawn.

"Carl Edwards. I'm a researcher here with the Shifter program. I have a particular interest in the bond Shifters share with their Agents."

I look up at him over the rim of my coffee mug, making a point to really look at him for the first time. A researcher with the Shifter program. I guess it's a good thing they've graduated me from being questioned by Agents to being questioned by scientists.

He looks as tired as I feel, with his hair standing up in every direction and dark circles under his eyes. But his curiosity is palpable. It makes me wish I could tell him everything and get his opinion on what's really happening with Chase. With the entire Shifter program.

But even though it seemed Agent Bates knew what Chase had done, it doesn't appear that he told anyone about his suspicions. As far as the Protectors and BioSol know, Bates' Shifter turned on him to protect me, then fled. And that's all I saw. No one has any idea where he went, or that there's a connection between my recent weekend fling and the attack.

The lying should probably bother me, but it's the least I can do ensure Chase stays free to be whatever he chooses to be. To have a life of his own, and a future.

"I'm sorry I can't be of more help." Lord, my voice sounds like death. I clear my throat, but it doesn't make much of a difference. "I need sleep. I don't want to go home, but if I'm free to leave I'll just grab one of the overnight cots..."

Disappointment flickers in his expression, but he nods.

Under other circumstances, I might have found a conversation with him fascinating. But all I care about now is getting some sleep and putting this all behind me.

I glance to the window again, and over the top of the flat-roofed compound, past the parking lot and security fence and wide, open field, is the edge of Morwood Forest. So many emotions surge inside me as I scan the distant treeline.

He's out there somewhere. Surviving and waiting as we use the only tool we know beyond a shadow of a doubt will save us: time.

CHAPTER 17

Future

"It was lovely to finally meet you, Dr. Chambers." I shake hands with the woman who's taking my place at BioSol, and not a single ounce of regret bubbles up to spoil this moment.

"You as well. Quite an honour. And please, call me Marilyn." Her handshake is firm, and her enthusiasm at taking on this position is palpable.

Not that it would have changed my decision, but I'm relieved to know that a capable, dedicated individual is taking over. And the fact that she's a woman makes me even more content with my choice.

Once I'm alone again in my office, I take a last look around. This has been the longest six months of my life.

At first, I was constantly looking over my shoulder. I was scared to death that they would find some proof that I hadn't told them the whole truth.

Then, it was the fear that any day I'd learn they'd found Chase.

But the last few weeks a new kind of fear has crept in. What if he's changed his mind? What if the way it felt when we were together was just a product of the newness and forbidden lust?

We've been apart longer than we were ever together. What if...

"Hey, Fate. What do you think of the new girl?"

Now that's something I'm going to miss about this place.

"New *girl*?" I give Matthew what I hope is a stern look, but it's hard to keep a straight face when he's looking at me with that boyish, dimpled grin of his. "Marilyn's well qualified and eager. She'll be a great addition to the Shifter program."

"Come here," he says, and that's all the warning I get before he's pulling me into the biggest bear hug I've ever received.

Wow, this man is huge.

When he lets me go, I'm blinking back a mess of emotions. I already miss him. I haven't told him anything about Chase, and considering he used to be my go-to person for girl-talk, it's been rough keeping that secret from him.

But he's still going to be working here after I leave. He's even talked about returning to the Academy to try for Agent status. The last thing he needs is for me to wrap him up in this deception.

"I'll miss you, Matthew. I truly will."

He nods, his eyes getting misty. "We'll keep in touch, okay? That's not optional."

I agree with him and give him one more quick hug before saying my final goodbyes.

But as I pull out onto the open highway, with my past behind me and my future getting closer by the moment, the only emotion I feel is anticipation.

One call, that's the only contact I've had with Chase. A month after he left, he called me from a bar somewhere in Moridian.

To anyone listening, it would have sounded like a random wrong number. But I hopped in my car for a quick grocery pick-up and called the number back from a burner comm I'd been keeping for just that moment.

I don't know if anyone was actually listening to my calls or tracking my behaviour, but I wasn't planning to take any chances on one misstep destroying everything.

But it's been six months.

Six months of career counselling, therapy, and long talks with my boss. Sometimes I feel guilty about it; The trail of white lies needed to pave the way for my departure from BioSol to seem like the inevitable result of the trauma I experienced that night.

But mostly, I feel alive. I feel like for the first time ever, my future belongs to me and only me.

I pull up to the motel, its weathered façade showing signs of disrepair, crumbling bricks and a lop-sided vacancy sign a testament to the misfortune many businesses in this area suffered when the new highway went in.

Not far from here is a winding strip of country road, it's pavement equally neglected, leading to a dead end at a sleepy town surrounded by endless acres of farmland. A sleepy town where not much happens, no one passes through, and an aging veterinarian had nearly lost hope that someone would ever be willing to buy his practice and honor his relationships with the locals.

A country clinic. Exactly as I'd always imagined.

I park the car and step out, taking a deep breath of the cool, evening air that smells like hay, and livestock, and possibility. The horizon is glowing with the pastel hues of fading sunlight, but I glance at it only briefly before my eyes land on something far more breathtaking.

CHAPTER 18

Chase

The moment she sees me, everything falls into place. My life, my purpose, my reason for existing in this world that would rather destroy me than acknowledge I even exist.

She pushes her car door closed with a dull thud, and I start walking across the distance between us. This cracked, dusty parking lot is the last obstacle, the last barrier between all the moments that came before, and all the moments ahead. Moments I'll share with her.

I fight the urge to run to her. Instead, I count every step until mere inches separate us. Until I can hear her breath, see the pulse racing in her neck, smell the subtle but intoxicating scent that's exactly as I remember.

"Fate."

Her name on my tongue feels like... like fate. From the moment she first touched me, the moment I first looked into those eyes as blue as a stormy sky. I knew she was the answer even before I knew the question.

I reach out to touch her cheek. Soft skin greets my fingers, and she leans into my touch, a sigh on her lips as her eyes flutter closed.

"I can't believe we're here. Is this really happening?"

I know how she feels. I've been in awe of every glance, every touch, every moment she gave me. And the past six months have only amplified that feeling.

I was nothing. I was a weapon, a mere accessory to a man who valued my life only so much as I could serve his purpose. Jon had about the same amount of concern for his own species, too. He used the people around him, took advantage of those who were weaker, and enjoyed inflicting suffering whenever opportunity struck.

Then I met my Fate. She looked at me, touched me, spoke to me like no one had since that lost girl at the carnival. I wanted to know everything about her. I wanted to talk to her. It was that desire that compelled me to attempt the shift to human form. Once I got a grip on the thoughts and emotions surging in my heart and mind, I knew without a doubt that there was so much more to life than I'd ever considered.

"I want to kiss you."

She nods her head as a smile lights her face, and I take her mouth. Gently at first, because I want to be sure she's really sure. About me, about us, about walking away from the life she had. But when she grips my shirt, pulling me closer as her tongue flicks across my lower lip, I stop holding back.

I kiss her like I've been wanting to since the moment we parted. Rough, demanding, consuming. Her hands claw at my back, under my shirt, and her hips press against mine, seeking out my cock that's already hard as steel and begging to be inside her.

Fuck catching up. I want her now.

I grip her ass and lift her off the ground. She wraps her arms around my neck and her legs around my waist, giggling and nipping at my skin as I carry her to the little room I've been renting by the night. The musty air, small bed, and flickering lights aren't exactly the setting I'd like for our reunion, but she doesn't seem concerned by those details. The moment the door slams behind us, she's tearing at my clothes like she's as eager to join with me as I am with her.

I want to take it slow. I want to reacquaint my tongue with every inch of her soft skin before making love to her the way she deserves. But when she wraps her hand around my shaft while pushing me toward the bed, it's clear she has other plans for how this is going to go.

With my back against the headboard, I slide my hands over her smooth thighs as she straddles my body and sinks onto my cock without a moment's hesitation. She's so fucking wet and hot and ready for me. She murmurs her pleasure as she takes the full length of me, her face a mask of ecstasy that mirrors the way I feel.

I don't know if she expects me to lay still while she rides me in this position, but that's not happening. I grip her hips and fuck her from the bottom, memorizing the way she looks above me, the sounds of pleasure and filthy words of encouragement that fall from her lips as I lift her up and pull her back against me in time with the pounding of my hips. It's fucking perfection.

I can't hold back my release any longer. I adjust my grip to reach that sensitive nub that's sure to bring her along with me. She must have been on the edge, too, because it only takes the slightest pressure to have her combusting on my cock as the pressure at the base of my spine erupts.

I pull her down against my chest as I empty inside her, my body lit up with the force of my release and my heart so damn full. I hold her tight as the aftershocks fade, feeling the ripples of her own orgasm as I soften inside her.

"I love you, Fate."

She lifts her head, bracing against my chest to look me in the eyes. "I love you, too. I love you so much."

We kiss, soft and unhurried. Then I carefully adjust our positions on the small bed so she's on her back. So I can worship her body like she deserves and show her how much I love her, and how grateful I am that she let me into her home, her heart, her life.

CHAPTER 19

Fate

I can't imagine a sweeter way to start the day, or the rest of my life, for that matter.

"Look," he says, his voice low in my ear.

I blink through the morning brightness to see the curtains are open wide, a vivid cotton candy sunrise painting the sky and bathing us in its warm light. The symbolism of the moment, of the beginning of the first day of the rest of our life together, grips my heart immediately. I push up to my elbow for a clearer view of the rolling fields and endless sky.

I glance over at Chase, but he's not watching the spectacular view. He's looking at me, his eyes reflecting the light and so full of love. I reach to trace his cheek, but he takes my wrist in his hand and kisses my palm.

"You've given me so much." His voice is a whisper, his lips never leaving my skin. "You gave me kindness, compassion, trust, love... you're giving me a life I never could have dreamed possible."

"You've given me all of that, too."

He presses his forehead against mine, and I wrap my arms around his neck, throwing my leg over his hip and moulding my body tight against his. Skin to skin, and it feels so right. Like his body is part of my own, like I was never really whole before.

"I found a house."

I pull back to meet his eyes, still alight from the glow of the sunrise.

"A house?"

He pushes up to his elbow, a grin on his face.

"It's not big, and it's a bit of a fixer upper. But it's close to the clinic, and the owner's eager to sell. I can do most of the repairs myself; I've been working in construction over the last few months, and I really enjoy it. I can learn what I need as I go."

I sit up, pulling the blankets over my chest to cover me from the morning chill.

"Do you really think it's the one?"

"We can keep looking if you don't love it. It's not exactly modern..."

His words trail off, like he's suddenly doubting himself. I kiss him quickly, unable to stop the grin on my face. "It's perfect."

"You haven't even seen it yet."

"I can see it through your eyes, and that's enough. It'll be ours. It'll be perfect."

The excitement returns to his features, and he dives into telling me everything about the house and his vision for how it will look once he's repaired, remodeled, and painted.

It's too good to be true. All of this. Him. Us.

But there's one thing that's been bothering me. It started with a small voice that I could easily ignore, but it's been getting more insistent over the last few months

"What about the others?"

Something flashes in his eyes, and I know he's been thinking about it, too. He slides off the bed, and I thoroughly enjoy the view as he walks to the tiny fridge and brings us back two bottles of water.

"Shifters."

The way he says the word tells me everything. We can't just turn a blind eye to what we've discovered. The others deserve to know what Chase knows, to have a life of their own and the freedom to choose.

"Once we're settled in, we'll find a way to help them. There has to be something we can do."

"We can't go up against BioSol. I won't risk losing the life we're making here." He slides back under the blankets, pulling me close. "You're the most important thing to me, Fate. I wouldn't do anything to put you in danger."

"Then we'll be careful. But we have to help some of them, at least."

He nods, and I feel the sense of purpose wash over me. We might not be able to change the world from our little country clinic, but we can save a few Shifter lives, and leave it a better place than the way we found it.

"I love you, Chase."

He throws an arm around my waist and pulls me down into the warmth of his arms as he nuzzles my neck and kisses my shoulder.

"I love you, my Fate."

I never could have imagined this is where I'd be, with my life turned upside down and everything I thought I needed tossed aside. It's fate, though I never thought I believed in such a thing. There's no other way to describe what I'm feeling now.

I'm exactly where I was always meant to be.

Ready for more *Shifters of Morwood*?

She's a lethal Agent. He's her loyal panther Shifter. When Whisper's devoted feline partner takes human form to save her life, will she fall prey to forbidden temptations?

Lose yourself in the seductive first romance from the captivating Shifters of Morwood series. Read Whisper in the Dark to light a fire in your heart tonight!

If you enjoyed *Fate in the Sunrise*, I would love it if you let your friends know so they can experience Fate and Chase's love story as well. And if you leave a review on Amazon, Goodreads, or your own blog, I would really love to read it! Email me the link so I can check it out :)

charleneperryauthor@gmail.com

I read each and every review I receive, and I adore hearing what you think of my work. It gives me confidence, motivates me to push through the hard parts, and inspires me to keep adding to the series you love!

Would you like to hear about my future releases and be the first to get freebies and sneak peeks? Subscribe to my newsletter at www.CharlenePerry.ca

I love to chat and am always delighted to receive feedback :)

Find me on Facebook! @CharlenePerryAuthor

Thank you so much for spending this time with me,

Sweet Dreams!
    -Charlene

Whisper & Damon

My name is Whisper. I'm an Agent. I'm the first woman who's ever made it through the Academy, and if you think that's because they went easy on me, think again. I challenged their testosterone-fuelled system, and I sure as hell didn't make any friends in the process.

Maybe one friend; my partner. My Shifter. With Damon by my side, nothing will stop me from earning the coveted rank of an Elite. But when everything I've worked for is within my reach, it all starts falling apart. Damon does the impossible. He takes human form to save my life.

***

I was created for one purpose; to serve my Agent. I've never questioned my life or my loyalty to Whisper. Condemning myself to insanity or execution in exchange for saving her life? It's not even a choice.

If this human body is unnatural, why does it feel like I'm myself for the first time? And Whisper... she's always been mine. But now I see her in a new light, and I want more. I need her to know this is who I am.

Can Whisper and Damon embrace their shifting reality, or will they be broken by forbidden temptations?

Read *Whisper in the Dark*, Book 1 in the complete *Shifters of Morwood* trilogy. Available now at your local Amazon and Kindle retailer!

* * *

9 798788 581323